The Life of Bosworth

THE LIFE OF BOSWORTH

A Cat

Maxine Handy

Maniot Books

Copyright © Maxine Handy 2007
First published in 2007 by Maniot Books
5 Orchard Drive, Little Leigh, Northwich
Cheshire CW8 4RW

Distributed by Gardners Books, 1 Whittle Drive, Eastbourne, East Sussex,
BN23 6QH
Tel: +44(0)1323 521555 | Fax: +44(0)1323 521666

British Library Cataloguing in Publication Data
A catalogue record for this book is available from the British Library.

ISBN 978-0-9553633-0-6

Typeset by Amolibros, Milverton, Somerset
This book production has been managed by Amolibros
Printed and bound by The Lavenham Press Ltd, Suffolk, UK

The Greeks believed that there is poetry in writing of something which is impossible and yet saying nothing but what is true.

Dedicated to 'Hendrix'

(born June 2005, died 21st December 2005, aged six months)

beloved Cat of
Hannah Grimward

CONTENTS

FOREWORD

*I*n this, his testament, Bosworth expresses inherent knowledge of his exalted position – indeed of the Exalted Position of *CAT*. The word serves as noun, pronoun and collective noun; but the mystical title CAT denotes a *Being* – omniscient, far-seeing, and possessed of ancient wisdom. In Ancient Egypt, CAT was a deity; although in the eighteenth-century poet Christopher Smart's *Jubilate Agno*, an essentially Christian vision, Jeoffry is regarded as a high-ranking servant of God:

> *For I will consider my Cat Jeoffry.*
> *For he is the servant of the Living God, duly and daily serving him.*
> *For at the first glance of the glory of God in the East he worships in his way.*
> *For this is done by wreathing his body seven times round with elegant quickness*
> *For he knows that God is his Saviour.*
> *For God has blessed him in the variety of his movements.*
> *For there is nothing sweeter than his peace when at rest.*

*For I am possessed of a cat, surpassing in beauty, from whom
I take occasion to bless Almighty God.*

'CAT' and 'GOD' evoke parallel mysticism and ineffability.

Combining Smart's Christian vision with the ancient Egyptian
could be said to place CAT in rank equal to the angels. Almighty
God alone can be the object of CATS' adoration. Certainly,
we humans are unworthy of their worship. We simply exist
to Serve – which, of course, lovers of CAT have always known
and been glad to know.

In truth, CAT knows All. Bosworth's knowledge transcends
the world of high European culture. Touching on mysticism,
including that associated with the male high voice –
countertenors and castrati (but significantly he doesn't dwell

on castrati for long!), he makes mention of those unearthly timbres and high pitch, linking them inevitably with those of CAT. Bosworth is assisted by his attentive scribe, Maxine Handy, whose own deep perceptions embrace such things. Yet while he refers to the composer Benjamin Britten, he fails to mention the composer's setting of *Jubilate Agno* (the cantata, *Rejoice in the Lamb*) which includes the celebrated CAT passage above. Given the counter-tenor/CAT link, could this Omission be through Displeasure that Britten not only sets the solo for a treble, but allocates the next one—about the mouse—to a counter-tenor? Perhaps.

Whatever the case, as in all things, CAT are not required to account for themselves or their actions. They may occasionally deign to explain.

Peter Giles
Counter-tenor and lover of CAT

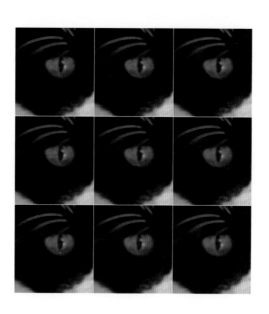

Little Leigh places of interest

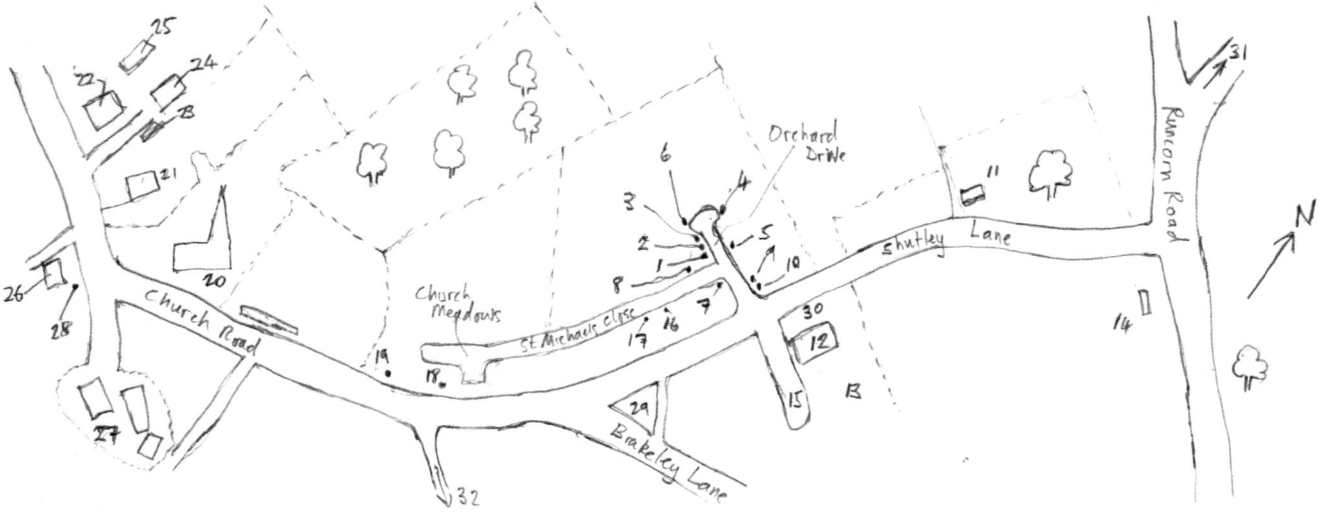

N

Runcorn Road

13

14

Shutley Lane

11

Orchard Drive

4
5
7
10
6
3
2
1
8
16
17

30
12

13

15

St Michaels Close

Church Meadows

29

Brakeley Lane

19

32

20

Church Road

24
8
25
23
21

18

26
28

27

1   Boz's house

2   Andy & Cherry, Jon & Sarah

3   Madman's house

4   Jenny Jones' house + dog

5   West Highland Terrier's house
    (Mr &Mrs Nice)

6   Rabbit hutch house

7   Trevor's house + ducks

8   Vic's house + Bryn

9   Debbie & Muj (formerly the Rae house)
    two BMWs, no cats yet except me

10 Labrador dog on corner

11 Thatched cottage + pond

12 Little Leigh Primary School

13 School playing field

14 Shutley Farm

15 Playing field + swings

16 Rosie's house – Tom's old haunt

17 Christine, Ian & Michael's house
    + Roger the cat

18 Joan Williams' house (multiple cats)

19 Sue and Dick's house (petless)

20 St Michael & All Angels Church

21 Vicarage with secret passage

22 Church Farm – Bosworth's birthplace

23 Barn

24 Stable block

25 Hay barn

26 Post Office & Village Hall
    (former school founded by Lord Leigh)

27 Horton's Farm + webcam

28 Trees & grass where I listened in

29 Grass area

30 Front entrance to school & garden

31 Road to luxury cattery (Blue Grass)
    + many farms

32 Bridleway leading to canal

INTRODUCTION

I was advised against using a first-person narrative. After *all,* this device has been rather done to death by the American author Alice Sebold in *The Lovely Bones*. Her heroine is writing from heaven, and many people in the United States took the book as proof of an afterlife, but I am not writing my memoir from the next world – not yet, anyway. In fact, I cannot be said to be

'The Writer' by Giancarlo Neri

writing at all – I'm using a human companion to dictate to and she is creating my incredible manuscript which will, in a different way, test belief. *The Writer* – Giancarlo Neri's nine-metre high sculpture of a desk and chair is currently exhibited on Hampstead Heath. It captures the loneliness, sacredness, and force of my, the writer's vocation, as does the poem by W H Auden, 'At the Grave of Henry James':[1]

> All will be judged. Master of nuance and scruple,
> Pray for me and for all writers, living or dead:

I am a truly exceptional *feline,* able to read, and talk to some very special *homo sapiens,* but not, as yet able to hold a pen or strike a keyboard. Indeed, reader, although by your standards I am only half-way to literacy, I'm proud to be a CAT, and I don't want to move too closely towards human acquisitions and characteristics lest I lose my connection to my ancestors and their talents. My unique skills mean that I have reached the pinnacle of feline development and evolution. Or have I evolved beyond the feline? Am I in fact divine? Perhaps I resemble the Greek sun-god Apollo, 'whose eyes and ears miss nothing in the world'. My closest cat relation is the glossy male tiger, magnificently marked, and seemingly much more impressive than little me, but in the forest of my dreams I am a predator of the soul. I use humans to document my achievements and to serve my purpose.

One of the most important functions of my book is to educate readers, especially the young ones, through my interest in high European culture. As a young man Henry James was described as 'a citizen of the James family'. When he became a famous author and European American he left behind this provincial identity and changed into the intellectual and aesthetic property of all people capable of reading and understanding him, and I aspire to a similar destiny. Access to educated conversation, books and the internet has developed a precocious mind, and I invite my audience to expand its knowledge by pursuing and exploring all references and allusions in this small narrative. My aim is the opposite of a current blockbuster, verbose and vacuous, which invites the reader to think himself clever because he is able to 'solve' illusory hidden clues and codes.

The American, Dan Brown, offers a simplistic, conspiracy theory view of European art, quite unlike that of Henry James. Writing on the experience of seeing Leonardo's *The Last Supper* (before restoration), Henry James described it thus: 'Only a shadow remains but that shadow is the soul of the artist.' Looking at the same beautiful fresco, all Brown can see in the poignant figure of John, leaning away from Christ in a gesture prefiguring their separation, is a cover-up for Mary Magdalene. I acknowledge that Dan Brown's book is rooted in European culture and history, but look at his 'treatment', as Henry James would have said, in horror!

Like the teacher who inspired Muriel Spark to create Miss Jean Brodie, I'm unashamedly elitist. The great singer, James Bowman CBE, who described my scribe as 'a pearl amongst swine', once said to her, 'Most people, Maxine, are perfectly ghastly.' I have read Peter Giles' magnum opus *The History and Technique of the Counter-Tenor*; he has been accused of elitism in championing the survival of the all-male traditional Cathedral Choir through his organisation the CTCC (Campaign for the Traditional Cathedral Choir). I too believe that only some people are worth taking notice of; I'm not addressing 'the duffers'.

> All the arts – music and painting and the written word – are by their very nature elitist, which is why they have such power to enrich our lives.[2]
>
> Beryl Bainbridge

Leonardo da Vinci was one of those rare people for whom no barrier existed between the human and animal domain. He respected the non-human part of life on earth and was a devoted vegetarian. Animals were a huge part of Leonardo da Vinci's life; he kept cats, horses, dogs, and birds.

He bought caged birds at the market just to be able to set them free. Leonardo had a lifelong fascination with the flight of birds. If you look closely at his painting *The Annunciation*, you can see how the very realistic wings of the Angel Gabriel resemble those of a large bird. According to Sigmund Freud, in his monograph of Leonardo da Vinci, the origin of Leonardo's obsession with flight lay in his memory, phantasy (or dream) described in his Notebooks, of being visited in his cradle by a bird of prey which put its tail into his mouth: 'It seems that I was always destined to be so deeply concerned with vultures; for I recall as one of my very earliest memories that while I was in my cradle a vulture came down to me, and opened my mouth with its tail, and struck me many times with its tail against my lips.' I've had numerous feathers in my mouth, and don't dislike the sensation, but I would never ingest heads or feet. Those dinosaur-related bird feet are slightly repulsive, and put me in mind of feeling queasy when watching Spielberg's *Jurassic Park*, where dinosaur feet seemed to be overly prominent.

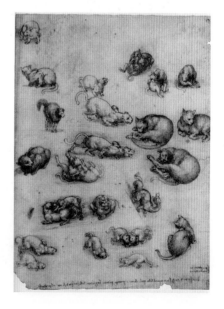

Many trusted cats were attached to Leonardo's studio and feature both in early and late drawings, such as the

Madonna and Child with a Cat, and the famous page of Cats (1513-16), in the Queen's collection at Windsor.

> *'You will speak with animals of every species, and they*
> *will speak with you in human language.'[3]*
> *Leonardo's Notebooks (1478-1518)*

I've looked at Leonardo da Vinci's Notebooks on screen. Like him, I am left-handed, (discovered when catching a bird in flight) and have had no trouble reading his secretive mirror writing. It is very touching to think of him in old age at the manor of Cloux, seeking sanctuary with his friend the French King, and never letting go of the paintings that meant most to him. He died in 1519. At Cloux, you can view his double bed, where he is said to have died in the arms of the King.

Leonardo's tomb lies in the late Gothic chapel of St Hubert, within the Chateau d'Amboise. His supposed remains lie beneath an inscribed plaque set up by the Comte de Paris, which, translated, says, 'In this place lie the remains of Leonardo da Vinci.'

The suggestion that I compose an autobiography has come from my many human admirers, although to be strictly correct, they anticipated only an authorised biography by one of their own species, like the wonderful *Charles – the Story of a Friendship* by Michael Joseph. I must not mislead you, reader; these admirers are unaware of my gift for the spoken word. This remains a quasi-secret between my female 'owner' and me. I think it unwise to reveal so unusual a talent; it might have exposed me to unwanted media attention and dangerous curiosity. The posthumous publication of my book will license the disclosure of my formidable intellectual and aesthetic talents. It will bring me back from the dead and honour my memory.

HOW TO TALK TO YOUR CAT

Listen! Your cat is talking to you – your cat is telling you how much she loves you. Watch! – the special friend who shares your life has so much to say to you about their feelings and needs... if only you knew how to listen and what to look for.

Open up a whole new communication between you and your pet... to interpret your cat's meows, facial expressions and often intricate body language, and

"Learn my language and let's start talking!"

My young mistress (the beautiful daughter of my 'owners', and my favourite person in the family) has always believed me to be capable of speech, and indeed, regards me as a *genius.* During my kittenhood and her childhood, she spoke to me constantly and seemed to be always awaiting a reply. Her natural empathy with cats gave her an instinctive understanding of so-called 'cat language', but so rapid was my learning that I soon advanced beyond ordinary feline sounds, facial expressions and body language. *We* had no need of a new guide *Your Talking Cat*, a working manual based on the primitive conversation available to the ordinary cat and its human companions.

In a fable by Nietzsche called 'Cold Star', he says that the clever animals invented 'knowing' (das Erkennen) – and that animals like this are bound to get into trouble. 'In some remote corner of the universe, poured out and glittering in innumerable solar systems, there was once a star on which clever animals invented knowledge. That was the haughtiest and most mendacious minute of 'world history' – yet only for a moment. After Nature had drawn a few breaths, the star grew old, and the clever animals had to die.'[4]

Whilst it is true that I seek immortal fame through the written word, and wish to celebrate myself (this memoir, as I have said, is to be left after my lifetime and placed in the public domain), like Homer's 'swift-footed godlike' Achilles, I prefer life in the sunlight to glory as a lonely ghost in the dark Halls of Hades. A poetic gloom seems to lie over the character of the greatest Greek fighter, destined to fall in battle at the hands of a god and of a man:

> The tomb of Achilles in Sigaeum according to Pliny, was one over which no bird ever flew, so strange and ominous was the atmosphere which brooded over it.[5]
>
> Lawrence Durrell

When the soul of Achilles, the great runner, recognises Odysseus all he wants of him is news of his son Neoptolemus' deeds on earth. He wishes he could rejoin him in the Greek elements above. Before Odysseus can see the souls of the dead he must pour a libation made from a mixture of milk and honey, wine, and the blood of a sacrificial animal. The ghosts must have 'access to the blood' and drink it before they can speak to the living. When Odysseus questions his dead mother, Anticleía, she explains with 'winged words' why it is impossible for them to enjoy a longed-for embrace.

It is the law of our mortal nature when we come to die. We no longer have sinews keeping the bones and flesh together; once life has departed from our white bones, all is consumed by the fierce heat of the blazing fire, and the soul slips away, like a dream and goes fluttering on its ways.[6]

Homer, *The Odyssey*, translated by E V Rieu

I know that I have a great mind. Do I have a soul? In any case, isn't it time my lifespan was extended, by cryonics perhaps? I am Bosworth the beloved, like John the favourite disciple of Christ.

I've heard with some surprise that the late Pope John Paul II supported experimental work on the decapitation and freezing of heads. But if my head was frozen after death and then decades later revived by a libation of cat blood, I would awake to an afterlife on earth possibly without my memories and personality.

And in the meantime where would my spirit have been? I might 'return' to find my family all gone, and to be alone.

Some years before his death, Henry

Tomb of Pope John Paul II in St Peter's

12

James had written an essay 'Is there a life after death?' James did not believe in a physical afterlife, although if he could have chosen, he favoured an afterlife on earth. What lived on was what the creative mind had discovered and enshrined in lasting form. In one of the final sentences of this essay, Henry James wrote 'I reach beyond the laboratory brain.'

Before I proceed any further in my narrative I must just mention that as my background is highly literary (and scientific) and my 'owner' and scribe is a Henry James obsessive, I'm basing my autobiography on the tripartite structure of Henry James' famous autobiography written in his old age. Thus you will find:

- ✧ 'A Small Boy and Others' (my birth, infancy, and adolescence)
- ✧ 'The Middle Years' (covering my time as the local Primary School Cat)
- ✧ 'Notes of a Son and Brother' (my relationships with other Cats in the family, and my own descent into old age)!

Indeed as my story progresses, I closely resemble the ageing Henry James, dictating to his adoring secretary, Theodora Bosanquet within the sanctuary of the red-walled garden room at Lamb House in Rye. He and I frequently intersect.

When I look back it seems to me that Henry James was the most profoundly sad-looking man I have ever seen, not even excepting certain members of the house of Rothschild. His eyes were not only age-old and world-weary, as are those of cultured Jews but they had vision – and one did not like to think of what they saw.[7]

Ella Hepworth Dixon

Henry James

There are many such ghostly descriptions of 'The Master', which draw attention to what T S Eliot termed his 'merciless clairvoyance'. He used certain people as a 'resource' especially posthumously, wrapping them, as he said, in the 'dignity of art'. He 'preyed upon living beings', and, under the influence of his older philosopher brother, William, liked to believe that the dead continued to exist as pure individuals somewhere in the mysterious infinite of the universe. Like the writer Peter Ackroyd he had an affinity with the supernatural and seems encircled by a private pantheon of his dead, just out of reach.

Wall plaque marking the site of Henry James' garden room at Lamb House

His eyes were singularly penetrating, dark and a little prominent...My servants used to say: 'It always gives me a turn to open the door for Mr James. His eyes seem to look you through to the very backbone.'[8]

F M Hueffer

It must be admitted that Henry James was reputed to dislike Cats, because they might keep him awake at night! A dark rumour circulated in Rye that his rest had been so badly disturbed one night by a very loud Tom Cat, that he had gone into his garden in a rage and killed the Cat. However, Henry denied this most ardently and said that the whole incident had been a dream/nightmare; yet another of his strange hauntings.

And in support of his kindness and tolerance towards felines I offer the following 'Cat on lap' anecdote by his niece Violet Hunt, which shows that *cats liked* him despite a sometimes uneasy relationship.

Settled in for the afternoon, surrounded by adoring ladies, the recluse of Rye (Henry James) sat complacent, holding my last new Persian kitten between his open palms, talking animatedly to the Beauty, who could not talk but *looked*. He quite forgot the poor beast, which was too polite and too squeezed between the upper and the nether millstone of the great man's hands to remind him of its existence, and I dared not rescue it until the sentence on which Mr James was engaged was brought to a close – inside of half an hour.[9]

Violet Hunt

I have been amused by the recent rivalry between Colm Tóibín and David Lodge over their Henry James-inspired books, which coincidentally they were writing at the same time, with different publishers of course. I am not saying whether I prefer *The Master* or *Author, Author*, only that there is room for another. Henry James was called 'the Angel' by his mother.

Let Henry James be my inspiration!

Part One

A Small Boy and Others

BIRTH

My life as a village celebrity began in March 1989 at a nearby farm – not just *any* farm you must understand, but one which had been in the same family for generations – hundreds of years of cattle, horses, Cheshire potatoes (grown in the open air) and Cats…

Some malicious natives of this (genetically compromised) village have alleged that my origins are deeply suspect (as deeply suspect as their own!) – and that I'm the undistinguished product of a very ordinary black and white Moggie mum (Jess – as in Postman Pat), and an unknown 'past it' Tom Cat. Whilst it may be true that my father was spreading his seed indiscriminately and my birth in a stable was rather lowly, I was nonetheless born in a place where tradition was important but survival uncertain. Furthermore, my birthplace was enhanced by its dignified proximity to the Victorian church and vicarage (the latter inhabited by an Opera Lover). Indeed, there is a longstanding rumour that a secret passageway beneath the ground links Church Farm to the austere, spooky old vicarage. Some of the 'inbred' native peasants deny this story, but newcomers are more romantic and open to the possibility of such a concealed route between these buildings of a similar date. I *know* that this connecting path exists because I have travelled along it and heard above me the sounds of a Handel love duet from his opera *Orlando*! Perhaps it was a love affair that first joined the two dwellings, the spirit of which still lingers.

From my formerly urban, flat-dwelling Mother (Stockport, I think?) I inherited City acumen, which mixed well with the love of rural pleasures and skills transmitted by my father. This combination has made me unbothered by traffic (except for one dreadful, near-fatal mistake in late middle age – which I will tell you about in 'The Middle Years'), and an excellent hunter, at home with difficulties that would daunt a less self-assured and obstinate Cat. (I hope you like my Augustan Antithesis and Anglo-Saxon alliteration – a device I've copied from Henry James who loved its English feel.)

My earliest experiences as a small Kitten on a Cheshire working farm included avoiding sudden death by tractors, cars, horses and dogs – plus a violent cockerel which befriended the farmer's stallion *Ace*. This aggressive bird was Ace's stablemate and passed every night roosting on his back. The farmer encouraged the bird because he was hoping to widen the gene pool available to his hens. Trouble broke out when gypsies who had been camping on land belonging to the farmer, and from whom the rooster had been 'acquired', returned to claim their allegedly 'stolen' bird!! He was concealed whilst they made their hostile but fruitless search – only to disappear from the farm some months later in suspicious circumstances. But I digress.

My protective mother seemed always to be rescuing me from

danger and moving me secretly and carefully to what appeared, at first, to be a safer place. Hence, from my earliest days I became adaptable and familiar with several 'homes' including a disused car, a damp cellar, and a lovely warm attic, which remained my home until I was 'given away'. In the words of the eighteenth-century philosopher Thomas Hobbes, life (at the Ford Farm) could be 'nasty, brutish, and short'.[10]

When the time came to leave my mother and siblings – and to be 'chosen' for a new home – my sister remained on the farm in the hands of a little girl called Amy (a close friend of my so-called owners' son). I felt sorry for 'Patch' (as she was unimaginatively named) as the little girl was careless and had a dreadful small sister who was emotionally disturbed and tried to drown a subsequent litter of kittens by flushing them down the toilet. Fortunately, the girl's mother intervened and rescued the kittens, but with the advent of brattish Olivia I was very glad that fate had removed me from the farm whilst leaving me within the familiar village of my birth and first few weeks of life. I moved on at the right time to avoid the rough-and-ready clutches of the three Ford daughters. Also, I've no illusions about farmers – Gerald Ford was very kind to domesticated animals but like all his fox-hunting chums he hated incurring vets' bills and did not regard farm Cats as pets. He thought of them as working animals required to earn their food scraps by catching mice and rats. It was rodent control or you were quickly made unwelcome.

We cats know that by bringing the rodent population under control, we heroically saved the human population from complete extinction at the hand of the Black Death. Ironically our black cat brethren were persecuted and killed in the Christian Middle Ages because superstitious humans believed that the Devil took the form of a black cat. In contrast, the Arab world has always chosen cats as the elegant companions of pious men and women, just as it has always embraced falsetto when intoning the Koran. I have no objection to being loved or tolerated for serving a practical purpose but I also expect to be honoured and protected for aesthetic reasons. In Albrecht Dürer's engraving of *Adam and Eve* (1504) I was delighted to see that there is a *cat* among other animals in the Garden of Eden. So we cats existed in the Christian paradise, before the fall of man.

I have my owners' daughter to thank for my early departure from Gerald's farm. She stabled her pony Amarilli at the Ford livery yard, and first saw me at ten days old when my head was misshapen and I was regarded as the runt of the litter (one boy and two girls). Although only a small child aged nine at this time, Tamsin was perceptive way beyond her chronological age. She realised that my head would soon assume a normal shape and that once I was taken to a loving, nurturing home with regular meals and indoor comforts, I would grow to be the biggest, cleverest, most handsome and finest cat of the litter. It suited me to be removed from my numerous relatives. Like Handel's *Semele* – 'Myself I adore'.

Tamsin's mother (my scribe) accompanied her to the farm when I was just three weeks old. Having heard a good report of me from her daughter and encouraged to have me by Christine Ford (the farmer's wife), she was eager to meet Jess's new litter. Apparently it was love at first sight, and I remember mewing frantically when picked up and held in her arms. I was sending out a kitten distress signal to my mother, as I was not yet ready to be separated from her, but knew that Chris Ford was eager to be rid of us. She tried to persuade my new 'owner' to take me there and then, saying that she was afraid lest I be killed by the dogs, or squashed by a tractor, but they resisted the pressure and came to a compromise. In my best interests I would not be collected from the farm until I was six weeks old. My new 'owner' would have preferred me to remain with my mother until I was eight to twelve weeks old, but realised that to do so would have placed me in peril from a variety of 'Ford' hazards.

My aristocratic 'mouth-filling' name was bestowed upon me by my present 'scribe'. It derives from her childhood infatuation with Shakespeare's King Richard III and his historical death at the Battle of Bosworth Field in 1485. My 'owner' was fascinated by every aspect of Richard III, and in her teenage years made an annual pilgrimage to Bosworth Field on the anniversary of the battle (taking with her a copy of Shakespeare's play to declaim aloud at the memorial cairn, in the style of Laurence Olivier). This stone was erected by the White Boar Society (Richard's emblem), of which my owner was a member! Also she kept a precious relic from Middleham Castle in Yorkshire (the maligned Richard's birthplace) – a tiny stone taken from a wall of the building and once used in a séance. My scribe was trying to find out whether or not King Richard had really murdered his nephews, the two little princes in the tower. She claimed that their ghosts did get in contact with her but were unable to answer that particular question.

Speaking of otherworldly things brings me on to a very sad series of deaths, which occurred amongst the feline companions at my home in Orchard Drive. When I arrived at number 5, after a brief journey from Church Farm (see the map), I was greeted by an exquisite, dark tortoiseshell Cat named Poppy. She had been the great friend of my famous, large black predecessor Tom, who had once climbed up the inside of a chimney and vanished for thirty minutes. When he at last descended covered in soot he left his imprint in several places on the new gold Wilton carpet at the cottage of my scribe's mother and father. It took numerous washes and rinses before his coat was once again clean and shiny, and he left no further outline of himself on the floor. Maxine likened this episode to the story of Tom, in Charles Kingsley's *The Water Babies*, a favourite book of mine even though Tom owns a dog, not a cat. Tom, the boy sweep, comes down the wrong chimney into Miss Ellie's white bedroom, and leaves 'the mark of his little sooty feet' on the hearthrug.

Tom   *Poppy*

My human family referred to Poppy as belonging to the idyllic 'Claybrooke Parva' days, on the Leicestershire/Warwickshire border. She was a rescue cat taken on as an urgent 'replacement' for the beautiful semi-long haired tabby, Moppy, who had been run over at the age of nine months. She had wandered from the safe and tranquil environment of her home in Western Drive and had probably been killed when crossing the nearby busy 'B' road on her way home for tea. If only she had been contented with her garden and the adjacent large school field. But unfortunately, at nine months, almost all cats are ready for wider horizons and seek to establish larger territories. Because, at this time, my young mistress was only four years old it was felt that another Cat must be found for her before nightfall of that same day. The family still had the legendary Tom who had once disappeared beneath the floorboards for two days during a central heating repair, but Moppy had always slept on Tamsin's bed and remained with her throughout the night.

Poppy was a charming creature and an immediate success with

the whole family. Tragically, at about six years of age, she developed FeLV (there was no vaccination available at this time). The elderly vet failed to diagnose the disease and my male 'owner' devotedly took her backwards and forwards to the vet for weeks of antibiotic injections and other treatments. She was suffering greatly with mouth ulcerations, cystitis and rapid weight loss, but despite these obvious symptoms of FeLV, the vet still omitted to perform a blood test.

I witnessed all this misery because as I had better explain, I was by then the companion of Poppy. My two predecessors had both been killed on the very quiet roads surrounding our house. Mosca (so Tamsin told me) was a spectacular, huge, black and white cat from a local farm on Willowgreen Lane (there are seven farms in Little Leigh). He came from famous ratting stock and was fearless. He was deeply beloved of my owners' small son, Leon, who aged five at the time, shared his addiction to playing in cardboard boxes. Mosca must have resembled the beloved pet cat of the last prophet. The cat was called Muezza, and was known for his 'valour, power and glory'. Every day, Mosca hunted in the nearby field and lined up his rat kill on the patio. Not only did he place them in a row but also disembowelled them — an average catch was between four to six per day. He never ate the heads; like the wise eighteenth-century cannibals, who thus avoided contracting CJD (the human form of mad cow disease). He was just like Beatrix Potter's Tom Kitten (except that Tom Kitten voraciously hunted mice only — because he was terrified of rats after being caught by the giant rat Samuel Whiskers). Tamsin read these stories to me.

Mosca was only about nine months when he was deliberately killed by a milk float belonging to the revolting son-in-law of a cat-hating neighbour. This neighbour was nicknamed 'Spongy' because he was always obsessively washing his car. When his elderly mother died in the geriatric ward of a local hospital, village rumour said that really she had died by the hand of her son, at home, and been buried underneath the floorboards. Such loathsome cat-haters are very rare in this delightful, friendly village, but this entire family was notoriously *horrible* and mentally unbalanced. They placed rattraps on the roofs of their cars in case cats tried to jump up and sun themselves, and they also drove at children playing on the drive. Our immediate (cat-loving) neighbours Andy and Cherry, who themselves owned two black and white cats (Holly and Pepper) made it clear that if any 'accident' befell their cats (such as poisoning or injury from traps or vehicles) they would hold these appalling fiends responsible and take direct action (murder). At a later date my female 'owner' asked Gerald Ford to give them a warning. Gerald was short but very strong (he could lift up a pony – no trouble), so having donned a leather jacket and pointed witch's hat (it was Halloween) he knocked on the man's door, grabbed him by the neck and lifted him from the ground whilst threatening him with violence if he ever caused any further trouble. This was the solution to our problem – never again did he dare to harm a cat – and indeed very soon afterwards, he left Little Leigh and the usual nice kind of people moved in. I've always known that fighting back is the only answer to bullying.

Gerald loved his land and thought it was his to do with as he chose. Another dispute with the nasty man at the house of the cat-haters concerned a complaint and threat of court action against Gerald for allowing travellers (those with the aforementioned cockerel) on his land. Apparently, the 'enemy' had been spying on Gerald by watching him all day through binoculars and then secretly betraying him to the council. If you've seen Nick Park's *The Wrong Trousers* with Wallace and Gromit, you'll get a feel for the dastardly plot. But, like Toad in Kenneth Grahame's *The Wind in the Willows*, Gerald also had his spies and friends in the right places to protect his interests. He was a drinking companion of our laid-back local policeman. So Gerald got away with after-hours drinking, driving very fast with excess alcohol in the blood, and using his shotgun to threaten trespassers. In fact he was so attached to his land that he didn't enjoy leaving the farm even to go away on a holiday, unless it was to Ireland to buy horses. Every day, Gerald liked to walk over all his fields, and said almost childishly that he would die in the same bed he was born in.

Alas, this was not to be his fate. A few years ago, after a mysterious virus kept killing his foals, resulting in a succession of stillbirths, and he was hit hard by the declining market for open-air potatoes, Gerald was declared bankrupt. He was so desperate for money that he secretly sold the magnificent, long, thick tail of Tamsin's section C mare, Amarilli. When Tamsin arrived at the paddock to saddle her pony, she looked in horror at the stumpy remains of Amarilli's once-glorious tail. The previous evening Tamsin had seen Gerald furtively talking to a strange couple who had come to the farm asking to buy real horsehair for wooden rocking horses, and overnight Amarilli's tail had disappeared! We all knew that Gerald had sold it, but he pretended to Tamsin that the two foals, who shared the field with Amarilli, had eaten it. Gerald's deceit fooled no one, and never again did we trust him.

It was all a far cry from the confident days when his parents had a thriving herd of milking cows. The Ford farm went up for auction, and in true country style was sold at a pub in a nearby village. Gerald's farming and hunting friends got him blind drunk and merry in mood before everything went under the hammer. What really broke his heart though was the loss of his favourite hunter, Drummond (whose noisy lip-smacking habit used to irritate me as a kitten) and his share in one of Michael Whitaker's showjumping horses, at livery on Gerald's yard. I think he would have killed for, or died for, that horse. In his youth, Gerald had been an accomplished show-jumper; I remember seeing the photographs of him taking high fences with ease and grace. His wildness expressed itself in his love for riding and he was often referred to as 'the black sheep of the family'. The auction at the Spinner and Bergamot public house in Comberbach resembled the sale of Michael Henchard's wife in Thomas Hardy's tragic novel *The Mayor of Casterbridge*, complete with wagging tongues, blame and prophesies, like an ancient Greek chorus. I commented to my scribe, Maxine, on the similarity.

The pub sale was a really rural occasion, akin to the Cheshire Show at Tatton Park in attracting local farming interest. To suffer such a fall in status and to be separated from one's land is to be disgraced. So despite the goodwill towards him and respect for his ancestors, Gerald really had no choice but to leave the area. From the proceeds of the auction, he settled with his family in Scotland in a beautiful large stone house with a salmon river at the bottom of the garden. He had always been able to cook good traditional food so decided to run the smallholding as a B&B. Despite attending a private school and making a minor recording as a boy treble soloist, Gerald was only semi-literate, so his wife did the books. He was still able to keep a few horses and ponies.

Nevertheless, this reversal in his fortunes was a bitter blow. A true non-tenant farmer, his own master and law unto himself, he hated to be separated from a place that was his world, and that he had expected to leave to his son and heir (also non-existent). As a descendant of the Ford farm, I share this feeling but have been lucky enough to spend my whole life as a respected eccentric in the village of my birth. Farmers in decline often become alcoholics wielding shotguns, or go mad.

Gerald was the Greek avenger figure, like Orestes in Sophocles' play of that name. Orestes, along with his sister Electra, took revenge on his mother for the murder of his father Agamemnon the son of Atreus. My young mistress, Tamsin, and her brother

Leon, have visited Agamemnon's palace at Mycenae in the Peloponnese and seen the monumental Lion Gate through which he once rode, as well as his sombre 'beehive' tholos tomb. The doomed house of Atreus was cursed, and I now curse 'The House of the Cat Haters', the evil slayers of innocent Mosca in my own Orchard Drive. Tamsin has an impressive photograph of her female cat Tayegi, superimposed on the Lion gate at Mycenae. Let it be a warning to those who deliberately seek to hurt cats.

The superstitious Romans were so afraid of the ghosts of those they had slain, that they beheaded entire defeated armies in the belief that this would keep the dead in the underworld. This would seem like a sensible precaution to avoid the Macbethian fate of the African dictator Robert Mugabe who, we are told, sits down to dine with the unbidden spirits of his vanquished enemies, known as 'ngozi'.

On 16th October 1590, the composer and lutenist, Carlo Gesualdo (1560–1613), prince of Venosa and count of Conza, brutally murdered his wife and her lover, and his second son, who was an infant, 'after looking into his eyes and doubting his paternity'. The terrible aftermath of this triple murder was that Gesualdo was tormented by remorse for the remainder of his life and gave expression to it in a single-minded devotion to his unique music, to which I Bosworth sometimes listen. I've also watched Werner Herzog's atmospheric documentary, *Gesualdo – Death for Five Voices*. Gesualdo is famous for the sharp dissonance and 'shocking chromatic juxtapositions' of his madrigal texts, with individual words representing extremes of emotion: 'love', 'pain', 'ecstasy', 'agony', and 'death' being given maximum attention. In his early years he had been a gifted singer, probably a counter-tenor, and a lutenist but after the act of violence his musical activities were also acts of penance. As he himself said, 'There is no witness so terrible, no accuser so implacable, as the conscience that lives in the breast of every man.'[11]

During his lifetime he tried to obtain relics, i.e. the skeletal remains of his Uncle Carlo, with which he hoped to obtain healing for his depressive mental disorder and forgiveness for his crimes. It was a common belief in Naples at this time that a human skull, if carefully tended and placed in a shrine, could be prayed to in the hope that its departed spirit might intercede for the living. There are many such bones in the catacombs beneath Naples. Gesualdo died without an heir, a virtual recluse in his forbidding castle, which you gentle reader might like to visit whilst meditating on the punishment awaiting a dark soul:

'Behold! Because of you I die,
And yours must be the torture,
Of seeing my death.
Ah, light of my eyes, alas, to my woe death comes.
Light vanishes from my sight. My voice fades.'[12]

(*Fourth book of Madrigals for five voices*,
1596, performed by the counter-tenor
Alfred Deller and his Consort)

Mosca had been acquired after the death of Tom, so following Mosca's sad ending, the first Ford Farm kitten (and my direct predecessor) arrived at No 5 Orchard Drive. Dear Kizzy was a beautiful smoky grey with orange eyes, deeply affectionate and adorable – but (so I've heard) after only a few months she was fatally injured by a speeding motorist on the corner road opposite our house.

This series of tragic events resulted in a *very brief* movement away from any further kittens – my family could not face the prospect of more loss and grief – so believe it or not an enormous whippet named Amy was purchased for Tamsin! This experiment was a disaster and after only three weeks this nightmare dog was returned to her owner (there to remain until the end of her days).

She was totally unsuited to being re-homed, as it turned out that her previous owner at a Newmarket racing stud had parted with her because she always walked around on her hind legs so that she could look into her mistress' pram and try to remove the baby daughter! When Brian took Amy for a walk by the nearby canal he said it was like being out with a kangaroo as a companion. Passers-by on narrow boats gave them very strange looks.

I feel that no more details are necessary to explain her fast-track return! I'll discuss the curse of dogs at a later point in my narrative; for now, I'll resume my tale of *cats* – because now at last we're back with *me* and my dramatic survival in a home which contained the Feline Leukaemia virus.

It was Tamsin's Uncle Mark (a GP in Kendal – and 'owner' of four pedigree cats, a Birman, Burmese [half-brother to our Oscar], Abyssinian, and a British Blue) who first suggested the cause of Poppy's dreadful illness. As soon as he heard the symptoms he gave his (correct diagnosis) and said that she needed a blood test immediately. This confirmed everyone's worst fears! The vet was deeply apologetic and genuinely distraught. Poppy had to be put to sleep at once, and not even her collar was allowed to remain. She was cremated, and her ashes are still upstairs in the main bedroom cupboard along with those of Tom Cat, the gerbils Oberon and Tytania (laid to rest in a special double casket) and Hercule, the ferocious hamster with an enormous mouth. I cannot now believe that I was expected to share my kingdom with rodents, my natural prey and antagonists. In fury, I once overturned the gerbils' cage, and Oscar was banned from Tamsin's bedroom for two years, just for attempting to 'wrestle with' Hercule. Our vet told us that as a child she had found her two gerbils being eaten by her beloved Burmese cat. The traumatic experience had affected her for life.

Fortunately, during Poppy's last week, her 'owner' Tamsin was staying with her cousins Kirsten and Kyla in Cumbria, so this distraction softened the terrible blow of her loss. But unknown to Tamsin I was declared by Doctor Mark Elliott – to be both 'at risk and posing a risk!'

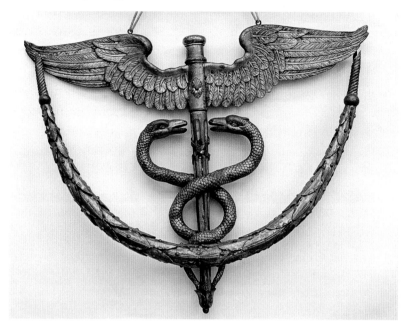

The Caduceus: Medical symbol of healing

He explained to my adult owners that the sinister FeLV was heavily present in saliva and could be active in a house for over twenty years! It was probable that Poppy had inherited the disease from her mother, and had been a carrier all her life. I needed to be given a blood test to establish whether or not this extremely virulent virus had been transmitted to me! The grim verdict was that should I be found to be carrying it I would place unprotected felines and small children at risk – thus testing positive meant being 'humanely' destroyed!!

The day of the blood test was sombre indeed – a life and death situation, which was beyond my control – I was at the mercy of vets, and human decisions. Given the virulence of the virus it seemed impossible that I had escaped infection – but my result came back negative! I must have had a spectacularly good immunity, which had saved me from contracting or being a carrier of this terrible disease. My charmed nine lives were evident from an early age.

After the tragic loss of Poppy and the reassurance that I was FeLV negative, two more cats followed in quick succession, and these are my present housemates – 'Oscar' (born 3rd January 1990) the sweet-natured, head-rubbing brown Burmese endearingly

Oscar

Seno

known as 'Osclet' or 'Flosc', and Senesino (born 28th June 1992) (known as Seno – or 'Skippy' by my male 'owner' with the beard) the neurotic, bossy, fluffy lilac-point Birman.

We all seem to be growing old together, and becoming slightly or gravely arthritic, although things have improved greatly in recent months. More on that anon.

The naming of our household cats is taken very seriously. Oscar belongs to my young mistress who named him (impressively) Oscar, Orlando, 'Arnie', because of his muscles (Arnold Schwarzenegger) Handy. His original pedigree name was Quernmore Remus, only brother to Romulus, who was later rumoured to have died in a house-fire. At the moment of choosing him, the smaller kitten of Ch Damala Straight Nochaser (sire) and Amahama Lintyar Belle (dam), we were worried that choosing Remus (who in ancient Rome was slain by Romulus) was unlucky and unwise. Sadly, at the age of seven Oscar became profoundly deaf, but of course, I have no communication problems with him. We send each other signals through scent, vibration, facial expressions and physical contact. I've always protected him, especially since his deafness increased his vulnerability to dog attack and road-traffic accidents. When he first became deaf, I always accompanied him outside and helped him with his territorial spraying. Having had the 'operation' to avoid contracting sexually transmitted diseases, we still fight rival cats over territory, but not sex.

We cuddle up together in cold weather, and he always defers to me in matters of feeding and drinking. His submissive attitude extends to washing my face and ears, although conflict occasionally arises over the matter of the human lap. This is an area that we both resent sharing – we demand exclusive caressing and other loving attention. I usually win this power struggle, but sometimes I become so irritated by Oscar's persistent attempts to remain in possession of a lap, that I jump off growling – and he wins! I then remain in a bad mood and sulk for hours – my own worst enemy.

The Birman, Senesino (named after Handel's star contralto castrato – his 'primo uono'), who sang the role of Orlando, is a very different matter. In general he is dominated by me, but he is a natural bully with very little intelligence, and sometimes goes for the full attack. He once fought with a neighbouring ginger male called Charles, and in minutes reduced him to a pile of ginger fur.

My personal view on Seno is that he is an unnecessary addition to the family, only suited to interaction with fellow thick Birmans, but the humans adore him for his beauty and dependency, especially my young Master, Leon. They have a truly special relationship – Seno spends most of his life on Leon's bed, desk, chair or lap when he is playing his Gibson 'Master/tone banjo or guitar, and is featured on his computer. What vanity! And now Seno has a male Birman 'friend' on Facebook.

The inconspicuous Cheshire village of Helsby, situated between Chester and Runcorn, has earned a

Leon on banjo

reputation for being the 'capital of bluegrass' in the UK: 'There are a lot of pickers around here,' say the enthusiasts. My own dear Leon now plays at their weekly meetings and is looking forward to contact with visiting banjoists from America.

Seno's love affair with sleep reflects that of Leon, who also spends most of his time sleeping, and is nocturnal, just like a cat! Leon has always said that he envies our lazy lifestyle and would like to have been born as a feline, in love with the night like the composer Benjamin Britten.

My favourite contemporary opera is Britten's *A Midsummer Night's Dream*. The role of Oberon, King of the Fairies, was written for the counter-tenor Alfred Deller, making use of the unearthly androgynous, but also menacing tones of the male high voice, with which I identify. James Bowman has enjoyed a lifelong association with this role, finally recording it in 1993. When James sings his aria 'I know a bank' he ravishes the senses. As soon as I listened to him I knew that he was a cat lover, and was not surprised to learn that he has two Abyssinians with spectacular ear-tufts, Max and Maud. As a breed Abyssinians seem always to be listening, whilst themselves remaining largely silent, the perfect cats for a musician.

They are also renowned for their hunting skills; James told my scribe that his little girl and little boy were always bringing him 'gifts' of mice!

Senesino's white hairs are a source of irritation, especially when they cover Leon's dark suit, but he only has to flop down on his back and flap his legs around to be forgiven for anything! His ghostly, pale grey mask and ears, which are owl-like, seem to be an endless source of human admiration, and his floppy body is cradled with delight, like that of a baby! He is imbued with the mystery, serenity and beauty of the moon. It is true that he hunts and fights like any normal cat, although I suspect his 'kill' has been killed by another cat, but, that apart, he belongs to a breed whose appealing qualities remain a mystery to any 'proper' Moggy.

Before giving you the details of 'The Middle Years' and my incredibly happy period as the School Cat, I must mention another traumatic death (human this time), and the role I played in helping the two children of the family to cope with their grief. I provided comfort, and a sense of continuity whilst also distracting them from brooding. It had been a difficult summer for them because mid-way through their caravan holiday in Wales (we cats stayed in a luxury cattery with curtains, in Little Leigh) their paternal grandfather had died suddenly and everyone had returned early to make the necessary arrangements. But far worse than the death of 'Organ Granddad' (so named because of his passion for playing the organ) was the terminal illness of their beloved maternal grandfather, known as 'Brindie Granddad' (after his Cairn Terrier). His condition grew worse and by the autumn of my first year on earth it was obvious that he was dying of cancer, which had spread from the lungs to his liver. He was nursed devotedly by his wife, but when she could no longer cope alone he chose to come to his daughter's family in Little Leigh, for what turned out to be the final week of his life. The house was decorated for

Christmas with a beautiful fragrant Nordman fir tree in the corner of the lounge, and a roaring open fire. He was made comfortable on the sofa, and was able to enjoy watching *The Snowman* for the last time.

Tamsin and Leon kept him company on the sofa and I joined them. Their granddad was pitifully weak, but he was just able to rest his hand on me and watch the children feeding me with my favourite chocolate buttons. 'Brindie' Granddad died peacefully in the early hours on the day before Christmas Eve, 1989. He was attended by his doctor son, Mark, and dear Dr R.O.C., the family GP who administered the morphine; he is another cat lover with two brown Burmese. I maintained my night-time vigil with all the adults of the family, and was there in the morning to purr at the children when they awoke to the terrible news that their beloved granddad had died. Everyone was suffering the agony of grief, but I helped them all to continue with Christmas by doing all my feline things – investigating presents, attempting to climb the tree, and batting decorations. I didn't manage to wee in the tub like my predecessor, Tom. The adults had become wise to this and ensured that it was covered and sealed with aluminium foil! Anyway, I was undoubtedly a stable and calming influence at this difficult time, as my Burmese Companion, although well meaning, was still very wild, and mostly interested in climbing doors and walls.

In Elizabethan times black and white cats were associated with melancholia, or so the historians say. I take a very different viewpoint, supported by the evidence of a wonderful portrait from that time, depicting the third Earl of Southampton imprisoned in the Tower of London. (He was a friend of Shakespeare, and the Earl of Essex, and implicated in Essex's rebellion against Queen Elizabeth I.)

The painting shows the Earl with his black and white cat, obviously his greatest solace during that terrible time of captivity.

Part Two

THE MIDDLE YEARS

*M*y life as the Primary School Cat coincided with Leon's arrival at the local school. He had already attended Toddler and Playgroup (taken there in a luxury Volvo taxi), but this had been in Acton Bridge, a tiny village a few miles away. Now that he was going to 'real' school, I felt that I needed to be supportive and provide a link with home (even though, admittedly home was only about fifty yards away). Also, Leon's schooldays gave me an opportunity to add interest to my own life and receive lots of extra attention from both adults and children.

Tamsin and Leon in 1991

So my almost daily presence 'down the road' was not entirely altruistic, in fact it was the beginning of a symbiotic, but ultimately celebrity relationship with the local residents. I became the 'neighbour' known to everyone in the village.

Tamsin was nine years old when her brother Leon started school.

One of Tamsin's very best friends was Michael Smith, the delightful son of Christine and Ian who lives just round the corner from my house. Michael's mum takes in abandoned cats, left behind when their thoughtless owners have either moved from the village or become 'too busy' to care for them. Michael's friends said that his mum, Christine, takes in stray cats and calls them all 'Michael'! According to Michael (who has grown up to be a biochemist, and banjoist, amateur instrument maker and artist), the cat Henry was his father Ian's best friend, and used to call for him. Henry would come to their front door and when Michael saw him through the glass he would say, 'Dad, your friend is at the door; he has come to see you.' Ian would open the door, saying 'Hello Henry, come in, love.' Sadly Henry has now passed on, having developed kidney disease in old age, but they now have Roger, the big black cat. The gifted Michael once observed that his father resembled a meerkat, but I think he looks like the composer Arvo Pärt who wrote the beautiful 'Cantus in memoriam Benjamin Britten'. Sadly the two musicians never met. Michael Smith also said perceptively, 'Bosworth has seen more than most.'

In fine weather I lay outside in the school front garden, beneath some trees, or sometimes in the side playground or rear large playing field adjoining the village park with swings, seesaw and climbing frame. My favourite season was autumn as I enjoyed chasing leaves, or being rolled in them by the young children at break times. At first I waited outside all day, until Leon came out, but later with my perfect sense of time, I accompanied him on his brief walk to school, stayed around for a short time, and then arrived early to wait for him and walk back home along Orchard Drive.

When the new headmaster (Mr H) took over, the school was transformed into a beacon of excellence, and I was incorporated into that process. For the first time I was welcomed into the school and allowed to spend all day in the classroom – I even attended parent evenings!! I usually dozed on the windowsill in Leon's classroom and was permitted to urinate in the flowerpots. Only one teacher, Mrs D was an enemy; she was a dull, religious fanatic and wanted me banned as an unhygienic distraction – this was nonsense! I was accused solely because she hated cats – we can spot this type a mile off!

However, I was warmly defended by dear Miss G whom Leon persuaded into kitten ownership. In fact it was she who termed Leon 'Cat boy'. And not only was I loved by Miss G, I inspired the headmaster to obtain two kittens for his daughters. Unfortunately, unlike me, they were not affectionate or lap cats – they were *not* adorable. But I cannot be held responsible for the disappointment of the headmaster's family – they were privileged to have known me. Anyway, the headmaster protected me from Mrs D's irresponsible plots ('I'm going to count to ten and then I'll explode,' she often said.), and I maintained my unique relationship with the school until Leon left to go to High School. After that I withdrew myself from the school environment, and was greatly missed by all, except for a few stone-throwing bullies ('inbreeds' I think), jealous of my lineage.

It was during 'The Middle Years' that I established a range of loving 'homes' for myself – perhaps as a substitute for the attentions of the schoolchildren, which although appreciated and enjoyed by me, had latterly become rather overwhelming.

I confined my wanderings to a small, select number of cat-loving premises. Other existing animals were no obstacle to my entry; wherever I go – I dominate! Indeed, one of my chosen homes was right next-door at the house of Andy and Cherry, and their two daughters. Andy once referred to me as 'the most arrogant cat I've ever met', and their large, boisterous, wheaten terrier, Ginny, lived in fear of me. When I was let in, Andy and Cherry would spell out my name, and say, 'B-O-Z is here,' because they dared not say my name lest Ginny the dog fled in terror. Despite all this, the two girls were devoted to me; I joined in their games, rode (dressed up) in their prams, and resided in their charming Wendy House (complete with a model squirrel on its roof). When I was ill after two knee operations, they gave me handmade get-well cards with wonderful drawings of myself! And, despite Andy's adverse criticism of my obstinate, persistent and inflexible temperament, he gratefully accepted a stone statue of me for his garden, to commemorate our relationship.

As you know, I have a car fetish, imprinted on me in kittenhood. The parcel shelf of a car is my idea of forbidden fruit. I wait hours for the return of a favourite car, hoping that when the door opens I can rush in and sharpen my claws on the parcel shelf. Andy was overly fussy, and refused to allow me to enter his car. This made me very cross with him, so occasionally I'd vomit at will outside his pristine front door. A mess on his doorstep might drive home my displeasure. It is often necessary to vomit – I use this device to 'train' my owner, especially in matters of suitable feeding. But sometimes vomiting is a sign of affection, as when done inside slippers. In my case, this is a very occasional gesture.

The house of Sue and Dick, and their four lovely children is petless, as stated on my map, but surrounded by a beautiful, welcoming garden where I have always felt relaxed. The youngest child of the family, a boy named Tim, became Leon's best friend throughout childhood. They first met each other in the village playing field, whilst still in nappies, and their close friendship centred on go-karts and 'Thomas the tank-engine' in every form. As young boys they went to London together to see the Egyptian Collection at the British Museum. Leon was especially interested in the mummified exhibits, but Tim was being awkward and said that he already had a 'mummy'.

The Fairclough family loved and respected animals but were often abroad and just too busy for the extra responsibility. Sue was no longer working as a midwife, but Dick had the hectic life of a judge. Although he does on occasion wear glamorous robes and a wig, he says the reality is nothing like the role of Judge John Deed, as depicted on BBC Television. But I admit that I do enjoy watching the programme for its clever dialogue in the courtroom scenes, and I fancy dressing up in all that scarlet. Says actor Martin Shaw on the role of John Deed: 'I've never done anything in my career that's been as popular with the public. People say, "Thank you for giving us something that treats us as intelligent." '

I seem to have got rather carried away with thoughts of the judiciary and more than a touch of red silk; I'll return to the story of Tim. As a result of Leon's influence, he started to express a desire for a pet of is own. So, for one birthday, Leon gave Tim an albino hamster, which he named Hamlet. Unfortunately, during some unsupervised exercise the small white hamster vanished into the Fairclough's very large cottage, never to be seen again. If *I* had been taken round to explore, I'd soon have found him! After many months of searching it was assumed that either Hamlet was enjoying invisible adventures, or his bones lay somewhere in the foundations of the house. This experiment with animal ownership was not repeated, but Hamlet was truly mourned. In the words of Shakespeare's Horatio, 'Good night, sweet prince; And flights of angels sing thee to thy rest!'

Another 'second' (or 'third') home in the village was that of the Rae family at the bottom of Orchard Drive, on the opposite side of the road (as indicated on my map 'Little Leigh places of interest'). This presented yet another challenge to my feline ingenuity as it already contained two hostile cats whose wishes I had to overcome. They were beloved of their owners, but were not going to prevent me from receiving a rapturous welcome. I simply ignored their ridiculous hissing and spitting, lavished affection on Mrs Rae and made my way upstairs to the comfort of her bed. Her own family cats, Oliver and Rosie, were criticised for being so jealous of the irresistible Bosworth!! Added to which, the firstborn daughter of the family was the best friend of my own young mistress who frequently slept there during her school and Sir John Deane's VIth Form college days. This household has a bearing on recent problems (now overcome), so I'll refer to it again at a later point in my story.

The household immediately behind my back garden is very much dog-centred, but nevertheless, I'm a favourite of dear Vic and Kay. I've always jumped down from the garage roof on to Vic's shoulder, and received a rapturous welcome. Now that I'm old and show no further interest in catching birds, Vic and Kay are especially friendly and often give me treats of fresh salmon. Speaking of fish, though, I used to get into trouble for taking an interest in Vic's ornamental fishpond. When he has been away, or simply not been looking, I've dipped into it, but when a fish goes missing he always blames the local herons. In fact, I am a hero to Vic because he once saw me stalking a heron that was after the fish in his pond. He was also very tolerant when, as a kitten, Oscar used his garage roof as one giant litter tray.

As well as herons we have ducks in the village, but Vic is fond of them. They live at Trevor's house, on the opposite corner to mine. In Shutley Lane at the entrance to the village, somebody has placed cones to which a home-made notice is attached. It warns motorists: 'Slow! Ducks in the village.' As I have said, my bird-hunting days are over but I admit that seeing these shiny, fat ducks so close up gets my teeth chattering in frustration at the sight of such desirable prey. Still, these quacking ducks are popular with the locals and seen as a village 'feature', so I don't want to cause outrage by chasing them. I pretend to be indifferent or even benignly looking on as they waddle past my door. The artist Tracy Emin says that 'birds are our angels of the earth' and expressed this benign power in her roman-standard sculpture, exhibited in Liverpool. But she still adores felines, and is devoted to her own cat, Docket.

Oscar got into trouble some years ago for having his nose pressed up against a near neighbour's rabbit hutch. They were some 'fancy' breed but Oscar did not care about that. The house adjoins open fields so he was able to arrive unseen. I watched him one summer dawn, his eyes fixated for hours on the wire rabbit run, waiting and hoping; 'when a god wishes to remain unseen, what eye can observe his coming or going?' Furthermore, we are now under surveillance because as well as a village newsletter, we now have a website and webcam. Leon calls it a 'cow cam'. All right I suppose, if you are interested in the WI or seeing webcam images of Farmer Horton's field. You might see a passing cow or sheep, or *me*. That's the great thing about life in the country; it is all about having small adventures. There are the seasons to observe, nature and animals at night; in my youth I've seen bats, badgers, foxes and hedgehogs.

Apart from visiting cat-loving households, I've also had my own fair share of problems with cat haters (human and canine). One such is my owners' friend, cyclist and former merchant navy man, Prussian 'square-head Mike', who, being infatuated with my scribe, pretends to like her cats – but we are not such fools and know that it is an act. I either keep clear of him and his two large 'mutts', Larry and Roamer, or deliberately annoy him by lying directly in front of him and blocking his way into my house. Such hypocrites infuriate me because they insult feline intelligence; we cats have supreme survival instincts – we know who is friend or foe.

There is an engaging true story about the very clever cat of the world's most famous seismologist Charles Richter. During the Californian earthquake of 1933, Albert Einstein was a visiting professor at the nearby Caltech. He was walking across the campus discussing earthquakes with fellow German Jewish refugee Beno Gutenberg, Caltech's leading seismologist. Approached by another professor who asked them what they thought of the ongoing earthquake, they replied, 'What earthquake?' Deep in conversation, the two scientists had not noticed trees and power lines swaying around them. When Gutenberg reached the seismological laboratory soon afterwards, he told the amusing story to his younger colleague Richter. On returning home late that same night, Richter was to be confronted with a feline perception in response to the earthquake that day, far superior to that of Einstein. Richter's wife told him that their cat had 'spat on the floor because it was not behaving properly'.

My relationship with vets (another group of scientific people) is ambiguous – can you blame me? We see them only when we cats are at our most vulnerable. However, I do have a hero within the profession of veterinary medicine, and that is Mr C Sale at the Willows Veterinary Hospital in Hartford. When I became lame from over-ambitious fence-jumping, he correctly diagnosed cruciate ligament problems in my hind legs. This is a rare injury in cats, much more common with footballers and dogs. Such an injury has just sent the striker Michael Owen home, and out of the World Cup in Germany. Using pieces taken from my thigh muscles Mr Sale repaired my knees completely and ordered six months' rest. This implant was a top job and is known as a

'ligamentus', like the one performed on Paul Gascoigne. The enforced idleness led to me having cystitis and other urinary tract problems, but my male 'owner', Brian, took me backwards and forwards to Mr C Sale until I made a full recovery. And visits to the vet have had their humorous moments, especially with Brian.

Not only has he been mistaken for Salman Rushdie (flattering?) but also Harold Shipman (not so flattering!) and most recently Saddam Hussein. In fact he resembles both John Peel and Steven Spielberg, but we have been announced at the vet as 'Mr Bosworth and Handy'!

B J Handy, BSc, PhD, AMIMA, AMIChemE, MInstP, CSci, CChem, FRSC

As if I would have been given *that* name!! It is even worse than being called Mr Sea-Sale by confused owners of *his* patients. The subject of his ridiculous name did arise once, and he good-humouredly blamed it on his over-protective, smothering mother. He complained that she still treated him like a child, and at Christmas time took him to see Santa Claus! His ridiculous combination of initial letter with surname was part of his possessive mother's strategy to ensure that he never left home or married. My young mistress would have sorted him out in no time! Anyway, he was a brilliant surgeon and genuinely loved, and was fascinated by cats.

Over the years I've had a number of illnesses including thyroid trouble (which gave me a tragic look akin to that of Henry James), and now in old age, chronic kidney disease. This means regular blood tests and steroid injections, but with the support of my wonderful new Australian vet Cameron Muir, now known as 'Cam', I've managed to avoid the horrible prescription diet, which Miss Smith, and other lady vets have attempted to impose upon me. The women are far too strict with me; they have rigid attitudes – I find the men far more relaxed and realistic. Cameron said to my 'owner' that what really mattered in my twilight years was contentment and an active mind. He thinks that a happy 'shorter' life is better for me than a miserable drawn-out existence eating the right food for a 'kidney cat' (as Miss Smith terms me). I don't doubt that she means well, but Cam gives me treats to eat on the examination table, and allows me to investigate his drawerful of needles and syringes. And after my injection he gives me *more* treats as I rub against and scent-mark his bare muscular forearms! Cameron looks very seductive in his 'greens' and is a flirt – he even flirts with his animal patients. He truly appreciates my remarkable intelligence and aristocratic demeanour. I wonder if it is because he is from our Commonwealth, and thus imbued with a sense of tradition? He says that England is the best country in the world because of its attention to animal welfare.

The most awful nights of my life followed on from a totally unexpected road traffic accident in late middle age, when everyone assumed that such risks were well past. It took place on the corner where poor Kizzy had lost her life. I simply mistimed, by a split second, a dash across the road, and was caught in the face by the dustcart. The impact broke my jaw and quickly put me into shock. My body ceased to move and I was just able to collapse into the adjacent conifer hedge. There I remained for forty-eight hours, completely hidden from view. I could see my 'owners' frantically searching for me and calling my name but I was unable to respond. I was 'dug in' in total concealment, and would remain so until the 'shock' subsided. In this 'closed down' state, I endured heavy storms, which covered me in wet earth. When at last, I was able to move I emerged from my hole and crept slowly home. When my owner greeted me she wept tears of relief and joy. Whilst she telephoned the vet, I rested gratefully in a shaft of sweet sunlight.

It was Mr C Sale who at once set to work on me; he said that being immobilised through shock had saved my life. He gave me painkillers, rehydrated me, and mended my broken jaw. It was completely wired with a large corkscrew structure protruding through my lower jaw. Within a few hours I was eating and drinking normally, and after six weeks the wiring was removed and a few teeth were filed down to ensure a perfect bite. Once again Mr C Sale had reconstructed me. Some years before, I had been 'dissected' in a vicious fight with an enormous Siamese cat. The wounds reached my internal organs, and Mr Sale had put me back together and stitched all my tears and lesions. He had had to shave off all my hair – so beneath my sleek black and white coat I actually look like Frankenstein's 'creature'. I don't like to recount this event because, obviously, I lost the fight. Fortunately, shortly after this attack that Siamese monster left the village.

I've explained to you how I protected young Leon at primary school and contributed to his childhood idyll. I've given him special memories and I've performed the same role for Tamsin. Oscar has frequently shared her bed; he is an adorable pillow companion and hot water bottle in winter – and goldfish brain Senesino, called Cecil by Tamsin, seeks out her lap and saltlicks her hand – but it is I who have acted as a barrier to predatory boyfriends!

As I explained in my Introduction, Tamsin and I have always 'conversed' at a sophisticated level. She has always appreciated my vocalisations, and now has her own highly vocal boy kitten 'Kambos' (Greek for 'forest'), a magical 'Meg and Mog' cat 'in his coat of fastidious black', along with her girl kitten 'Tayegi'– 'her coat is of the tabby kind, with tiger stripes and leopard spots' – who although very loving, does not seem to be as 'talkative'. She was found wandering and motherless at two weeks of age, so that is probably the reason for her limited vocabulary. The naming of these cats is very interesting and personal. Kambos' full name is Kambos SORT Handy, so called after the Sheffield Outreach Team for mental health, from whence he came at eight weeks old, rescued from one of their 'recovering' clients. He was given to Tamsin by the team at the conclusion of her two years of postgraduate training at Sheffield University. Initially, he was wrongly assigned female gender and called 'Kalamata' but the mistake was soon discovered, and his name changed to Kambos. Because he was never fed at his former 'heroin' household, he has a neurotic relationship with food and 'comfort eats'. He is now huge but timid, and highly strung. Tamsin tried to train him to walk on a harness but he had an idiosyncratic sense of direction which led him out of the harness and up a bush. Having spent his first weeks on dark carpetless staircases, he demands endless human interaction, especially arm-wrestling and string games. Brian refers to him as 'dark matter and dark energy', and credits him with knowledge of a cat's version of 'string theory'. Tiny Tayegi, the female cat, a ferocious hunter and washer of kittens, came from Mid-Cheshire animal rescue and is named after the Taygetos Mountains in the Peloponnese, in southern Greece. Tamsin and my scribe shared an unforgettable mother-and-daughter holiday there in a June celebration at the end of her studies. They stayed in the village of Kardamyli, home of the legendary Patrick Leigh Fermor, at the foot of the Taygetos where wolves once roamed and great eagles fly.

Old Kardamyli

My scribe has told me that her most idyllic moments on holiday with Tamsin were dusk in the olive groves and cypresses of St Sophia Monastery near Exochori, and a simple Greek shepherds lunch of olive spread, bread, fruit and walnuts beneath a mulberry tree in front of the church of Spiridon Theodori. 'This was eternity and I was sitting beneath a tree in Paradise.'[13]

Anyway, to return to Tamsin's would-be suitors, I knew at once whether or not they were right for her and indicated this through my response to them. Those I approved of were singled out for close contact and unobtrusive affection. Those I disliked were met with hostile body language and voice, and I prevented them from crossing the threshold to her bedroom.

I'm very sensitive to voices – and I know a great deal about musical sounds because I've always lived with counter-tenors, ranging from male high voices of plangent disembodied beauty, to those impostors who in the words of Peter Giles 'sound like the cat that's had its tail trodden on'. In the baroque period, the male high voice was synonymous with heroism and eroticism, but also identified with angels. For ten years my scribe has been writing a private memoir of the great counter-tenor James Bowman. The piece combines vocal music, painting, and literature as the three routes to understanding this genius singer. The title of the memoir is *Burning in Blueness*, and it is in three sections: 'The Voice', 'The Man', and 'The Memory'. The 'old master' frontispiece is Leonardo da Vinci's *The Virgin of the Rocks*.

A voice is a person, and if I dislike the voice, then I dislike the person. Tamsin has appreciated me as her ally and defence, and now that she has left home I know that her two young cats will perform this important function. They will give her their complete devotion, and guide her in choosing a lifelong mate.

Kambos and Tayegi

But I await the verdict of Kambos and Tayegi on Dominic. They are taking things quite slowly with her partner of five years, and former English teacher. Certainly he is excellent at playing with them, but he has yet to prove himself in terms of their physical care. Tamsin is waiting to see his readiness for emptying litter trays, feeding, cleaning up, and volunteering to pay the vet's bills. I have reminded Tamsin that when the time came for Neoptolemus, the renowned son of Achilles to claim his bride, *he* was given the task of crossing the Taygetos Mountains, and had to walk all the way from Kardamyli to Sparta.

Dominic with a Chinook helicopter

At present Dominic is away at base in Shropshire for most of the time as he is training to be a PTI in the RAF. Having completed basic training at RAF Halton, when he was known as 'Senior Man', in charge of a flight, he won two awards – top cadet and top shot!! On 18th July 2006 he will graduate from the School of Physical Training at RAF Cosford, winning yet another cup, to be awarded to him in the famous PTI museum quadrant that bears the motto 'viribus audax'. He is soon to take up a post in Lincolnshire at RAF Waddington and probably undergo further training as an ATI before moving on to RAF Cranwell. In January 2007 he is participating in the RAF leg of a recreation of Sir Francis Chichester's round-the-world voyage in the famous ketch *Gypsy Moth IV*, an excellent preparation for a commission. Tamsin, on my advice, is to settle for nothing less in a man than a commissioned officer. Flight-Lieutenant Clarke sounds much better than Corporal Clarke, and I love the word 'flight' for all the reasons I've mentioned. In crossing the dangerous waters of the Gulf of Aden, the entire team and their small, historic sailing boat will be at grave risk of attack by 'pirates'. These terrifying men are heavily armed and intent on robbery and kidnap. I know that any such challenge will meet an aggressive, determined and brave response from *Gypsy Moth IV*. And it might comfort our heroes to know that American gunships and marines are currently in the area, should rescue by the 'Stars and Stripes' prove necessary. I'll be reading Dominic's daily log and enjoying his stories and photographs; I hope to be piped aboard at Journey's End in Plymouth, before *Gypsy Moth IV* comes to rest at Cowes. Dominic is certainly approved of by me as an intriguing combination of athleticism, 'gung-ho' spirit and literary sensitivity, and is Yorkshire born like the animal-loving Brontës:

> Such a strong wish
> for wings.
> Such an urgent
> thirst to see,
> to know, to learn[14]

Part Three

NOTES OF A SON AND BROTHER

As a well spent day brings happy sleep,
So a life well used brings happy death.[15]
                    Leonardo da Vinci's notebooks

*C*heshire is known mockingly as 'the Surrey of the North', but in fact it now has more millionaires than Surrey. Some Cheshire people like to display their wealth and it is said to be the favourite county of footballers.

During a recent visit to Thailand by my young mistress Tamsin, the Buddhist monks she encountered were as interested in Manchester United as they were in meditation and caring for the wild tigers in their sanctuary.

At one time Tamsin had a boyfriend who was a highly talented footballer, and played for the England Under Twenty-one youth team. He twice proposed to her, only to be turned down. As the supreme sacrifice, he even offered to give up football for her. She rejected him and broke his young heart. His name was Ryan…

Tamsin stroking a tiger

Still, I could not imagine Tamsin as a footballer's wife obsessed with shopping in the Trafford Centre. We are part of ancient rural Cheshire; as I have said my village has seven farms and the remains of what were once large orchards. And, unlike Surrey, our landscape has retained its hedges.

As I've settled in to the third part of my life and been aware of the ageing process – arthritis, hyperthyroidism, and dodgy kidneys…my thoughts have frequently turned to metaphysical or psychic phenomena, such as happened to my female 'owner' just before the death of Tom. Maxine is obviously able to describe and experience events blocked from ordinary perception. Her experience of sounds and extreme agitation moments before Tom's death proves that the future can come into our awareness at an earlier time – a future event was sensed through precognition. With preternatural clarity she experienced Tom's deceased, invisible feline ancestors calling to his soul from their next world.

In Ancient Greece the mortal and divine existed in close contact. Maxine has told me of a Greek intellectual named Ilias, met with whilst in the Mani, who claimed descent from the Spartans and spoke of the old people from the villages as 'those who are soon leaving us and await our return'. This telling phrase revealed that the religious beliefs of Ancient Greece have metamorphosed into those of the Orthodox Church. The Greeks are at their ease with the idea of transitional planes of existence marked by sacred, often marginal, places like Cape Taíneron which has an entrance to the underworld. Orpheus descended here in search of his Eurydice. The entrance of the cave was occupied by a Sanctuary of Poseidon, eerily signposted today as 'the death oracle of Poseidon'. The sanctuary had a resident psychopompeion (escorter of the souls of the dead), and was one of the few places in Greece where a killer could summon up the soul of his victim and placate him with a sacrifice. In more recent times the psychopompeion has been replaced by the archangel Michael as a gatherer of souls. Local villagers have seen him passing in front of the cave by the small pebble beach, with his sword drawn.

When Maxine and Tamsin spent some time there in the ancient Greek ruins they didn't see any ghosts but agreed with Nikos Kazantzakis that 'nowhere else can one pass so easily and serenely from reality to dream'.[16]

The beach at Cape Taíneron

My male 'owner' studied quantum mechanics whilst at university, and often talks about my species in the context of a 'thought experiment' devised by some theoretical physicist called Schrödinger, involving his pet cat! Apparently, the experiment was supposed to demonstrate the differences between the quantum world and the everyday world.

Personally, I do not care for this experiment (The Cat Paradox), as it implies that I can exist in two states at once while I am not being observed. In Schrödinger's cat-in-the-box experiment it meant that I would simultaneously be both dead and alive, but of course, I know from personal experience that this cannot be true. Like Shakespeare's King Lear I am quite able to decide for myself whether I'm alive or dead. I know the difference. My 'owner' thinks that this experiment is a clever paradox, but I know that it is just faulty reasoning. John Gribbin, the author of *In Search of Schrödinger's Cat*, interprets it as a parable, 'a truth stranger than any fiction'. So, in that sense alone it does resemble my own book.

For some time my male 'owner' has had a keen interest in theoretical physics, and has been reading books on cosmology, string theory, extra dimensions, and braneworlds. I've also had the opportunity to study this new area whilst sitting on Brian's computer keyboard. I'm his favourite cat and he never restricts my activities, however inconvenient. One of his best loved papers at present, which I've read on screen, is 'The Speed of Thought: Investigation of a Complex Space-Time Metric to Describe Psychic Phenomena'. I was shocked to find him reading such a paper on the possibility of faster than light communication! Of course as a scientist he is only interested in a scientific explanation for allegedly paranormal phenomena. I do not understand the desire to rationalize these effects, as we all know that nothing travels faster than light.

Being a mystical cat, the explanation is quite obvious to me. All his life Schrödinger was hounded by people asking about his cat (even though the cat itself is an irrelevance – it was merely there as a macroscopic object). But ironically the only reason people were interested in his theories was because he cited a cat. Schrödinger's last words were reputed to be 'I wish I'd never mentioned that (bloody) cat.' Let this be a warning to future scientists! Not content with Schrödinger's cat, John Gribbin has written a sequel called *Schrödinger's Kittens*. A S Byatt described it in *The Sunday Times* as 'precise yet mysterious…as beautiful as a poem and as exciting as a novel'. With respect to papers written on quantum non-locality, it is unfortunate that modern physicists now refer to entangled particles as being in a 'cat state'. However, who would believe anyone who wrote:

'Consciousness is a singular of which the plural is unknown. There **is** only one thing, and that which seems to be a plurality is merely a series of different aspects of this one thing, produced by a deception…as in a gallery of mirrors.'[17]

Erwin Schrödinger 'What is Life?'

Schrödinger's cat

My response to the above is to purr one of my best-loved pieces of music, Arvo Pärt's 'Spiegel im Spiegel' (Mirror in the Mirror), simple, sparse, and seductive. Now that does express the mystery of time and eternity and has resonated within me for most of my life.

At least Brian's scientific papers have been connected with my own current preoccupations – but just recently they have been frequently interrupted by his addiction to *The Times* Sudoku. I see no relevance there to a Cat's afterlife – it's just meaningless squares and numbers. I preferred the days when he played chess with Tamsin. Although the strategy was irrelevant in my terms, at least it gave me the opportunity to weave in and out of the pieces, and create chaos by knocking them over. Also from the vanity point of view the black and white of the chequerboard matched my coat colour! My markings are superbly symmetrical, unlike the 'Friesian Cow' appearance of Kelly's cat Kia (a Jellicle Cat) who has a bizarre, wholly black tail.

> Jellicle Cats are black and white…
> Jellicle Cats develop slowly,
> Jellicle Cats are not too big;
> Jellicle Cats are roly-poly,
> They know how to dance a gavotte and a jig.
> 'The Song of the Jellicles', T S Eliot[18]

I mentioned earlier that my young mistress has now left home for a short period with her two kittens, and is currently living in a wonderful 'boho' area of Sheffield called Netheredge. But before this she revisited the Mani in Greece for four weeks with her boyfriend Dominic, and her new kittens were left here for her mother to look after. Kambos in particular took over the house and my so-called owners' time and affections. Also, although I have no progeny, he thought I was a male role model and father figure. He copied my every movement and jumped

Kia and Cassie

on my back to encourage me to play. At first I retreated to the hall and landing to escape these unwanted attentions, but when my special cellular blanket was commandeered, I decided to re-visit an earlier alternative home and teach a hard lesson to my owners. I reconnected with the former home of the Raes, now occupied by Debbie, a physiotherapist, and her husband Mujahid (Arabic for warrior), an orthopaedic surgeon originally from Baghdad. (I think it best to conceal the meaning of his name in general conversation in this village.) They simply adore me, and through determination, inflexibility, and the previously mentioned 'tragic look' (learned from my time with an underactive thyroid), I gained entry to both their hearts and their conservatory. The man was a bit tricky at first; like most doctors he was unhappy with my 'unhygienic' presence upstairs on the bed, but by following him around I gained his approval and concern. Cats in Iraq are highly respected. After death they are the subject of elaborate ritual in which the body of the cat must be placed on a bed of straw. It is interesting to remember that Benjamin Britten wanted his dead body to be placed in the reed beds at Snape, in Suffolk, so that he could dissolve into and merge with the sea. This was not allowed because of local regulations, but as second best, his grave was lined with reeds, by a local artisan known to Britten.

The treatment of cats in Iraq reflects their status both in Ancient Egypt and the Islamic world today. In Ancient Egypt the cat was a most important deity. 'The highest god, Ra, was sometimes addressed as 'supreme Tom cat', and in the 'Book of the Dead' the cat was also equated with the sun. Legend tells us that 'in times immemorial the sun god Ra, in the shape of an enormous cat, fought against and overcame darkness manifesting itself as a powerful serpent.'[19] (Annemarie Schimmel, *Cairo Cats*.)

The gentle cat-headed goddess Bastet was also worshipped; her temple was located in Bubastis in the Nile Delta. According to Annemarie Schimmel, 'the first story about the war between cats and mice (Tom and Jerry cartoons) originated in ancient Egypt, and was told and retold all over the world in poetry and in prose.' Great cat funerals took place in Bubastis and to show their grief people were  even known to shave off their eyebrows! The cat was buried just like a human being, and the owner often put some objects into the grave so that his pet could play with them in the other world. Little bowls for food and milk have also been found. When Leon was a small boy I remember that he was given a huge 'mummified' wooden cat as a birthday present. That cat had been wrapped in metres of white toilet roll in imitation of linen bands. As Leon unwrapped his bandaged cat he asked, 'Is it from the British Museum?'

Mujahid's fierce name belies his gentle nature; he is kind and compassionate especially to the vulnerable. He puts me in mind of Goya's *Self-Portrait with Doctor Arrieta*, painted as a heartfelt tribute to the much admired Doctor, Don Eugenio Garcia Arrieta who saved the life of the elderly Goya, and went on to study bubonic plague in Africa. 'The proximity of their two heads, the one so desperate and the other so consoling, implies that the help provided by Arrieta was as much psychological as physical.' The shadowy and sinister faces behind the two solemn people belong to a dark and frightening region, like the nightmare of Iraq. Members of Muj's family are in great danger in Baghdad; they are having to flee to Syria leaving their possessions behind them. One of his brothers has been threatened with beheading. Muj says that Iraq has been destroyed by the invasion and resulting war. Tribal and religious divisions have been unleashed with terrifying consequences.

Also, as I suffer from joint problems, can you think of a better combination of expertise than Debbie and Mujahid for my unofficial massage treatment?

Muj and Debbie on their wedding day.

And Debbie might try out some alternative therapies on me – like acupuncture, and sweet smelling essential oils and herbs. I wonder if she has catnip in her collection! I hope so. The ancient Egyptians groomed and bathed their cats, anointed them with fragrant oils and fed them with excellent food. Can I therefore expect this same pampering at the house of Debbie and Muj? Debbie believes that I'm inhabited by the spirit of her dead grandmother. Apparently, I first appeared at Debbie's window, with my nose pressed against the glass, on the very day after her beloved grandma had died. Thus recently bereaved and in mourning,

Debbie is comforted by my presence. She says that I have the most expressive eyes she has ever seen.

Women seem often to have a very special relationship with their cats. In the nineteenth century the caravans of pilgrims going from Cairo to Mecca often took cats, both for rodent control and because of the prophet's love for cats. These Egyptian cats were looked after by a woman, known as the 'mother of cats'. I think that Tamsin is just such a maternal icon for cats.

For many months I bore a tremendous grudge towards my owners for allowing the intrusion of Kambos and Tayegi. I'd still purr for Leon and his then girlfriend Kelly, even though her two kittens, Cassie (a spectacular Bengal) and Kia, occupied my lounge for more than a week – but I would not purr at, or make eye contact with Maxine. I decided to make her worry about me and suffer rejection, as I had done. The problem was that she had told Debbie not to feed me, so that I had to return home for food. However, I also made use of another previous home – that of Andy and Cherry, now occupied by two teachers Jon and Sarah (who rescued me when I was locked in the garage). They too accept and adore me, especially Sarah who calls me 'darling'. Jon is a little more abrupt, but Sarah is in control of the situation and indulges me.

Whether or not I would ever forgive my owners their betrayal I was still unsure. My companions Oscar and Seno were entirely back to normal, having reclaimed the lounge and their goose-down cushions, but I'm a much more complex character, and as yet my grudge was still burning… .Whilst I was able to negotiate fences, oil tanks, and cotoneaster bushes I had the freedom to change my location. And I could still catch prey, including rabbits (Brian recently buried one of mine in the garden). My flexibility remained excellent – I could stick fast and then stretch like an elastic band before returning to the original place. I relented a little towards Brian – after all, when he unknowingly locked me in his car overnight, I had the pleasure of weeing in the car well, and he did not seem to mind at all. He found it amusing!

Then a change began to take place inside me. The weather turned autumnal, sometimes wintry. The mornings and evenings were damp and chill. To my astonishment I found myself in the lounge, seated on Maxine's lap, drooling and affectionately nipping her wrists and knees! Such was my relief that the kittens had finally gone that my trust was beginning to return. Perhaps my owners had been punished enough…perhaps the time had come to return home permanently…

As Christmas 2005 (and my seventeenth birthday) approached I began to experience the pull of my earlier life within the loving family. Some beneficent force was drawing me closer to the delights of sharing the warm sofa with all the other cats, being handfed Maltesers by Brian, and once again sleeping at the bottom of Tamsin's bed. I was already looking forward to the arrival of Brindie Grandma's 'Torah' the dachshund; it was my responsibility to monitor her activities! I keep her away from the cat food and ensure that she does not bite Senesino's bottom. I rediscovered a sense of purpose and enjoyed being in control. My dominance was restored, noticed and praised by our many visitors. These renewed activities would keep me young. At my most desolate I had felt like John Clare the Northamptonshire 'peasant poet' during his Journey out of Essex.

> 'I soon began to feel homeless at home…though my home is no home to me my hopes are not entirely hopeless'[20]
>
> Glinton 27th July 1841

But now I've returned home permanently and taken over the radiator hammock in the lounge. Also Cameron has done further five-day thyroid tests and is now successfully treating my overactive thyroid. I hope to gain weight and am certainly feeling much less 'toxic'. After a dark, hard journey, I am re-established within my family – like Odysseus in Homer's *Odyssey*, who was promised a peaceful old age and 'gentle death' by the Theban prophet Teiresias.

I'm still keeping in intermittent touch with the place of my temporary exile. I was introduced to Debbie and Mujahid's family who had arrived for Christmas and given a celebratory plate of chicken, despite a ban by Muj for twice urinating in the lounge. It was his fault because he did not get out of bed at three a.m. to let me out. I made it quite clear by high-pitched noises that I needed to empty my bladder. Because of his demanding morning operating schedule, Muj objected to being disturbed at night. My mistress advised him to have an afternoon 'cat nap' (during his tea-break) but he was unfamiliar with the term and concept! He admires Senesino because he is 'fluffy and falls on his back at a touch', but did confuse his name with what he thought was a discussion on 'septicaemia'. This confusion over Seno's name gave me a malicious thrill. I now only visit them like the Cheshire Cat from *Alice in Wonderland* who 'manifested itself, communicated with Alice, and then disappeared'.[21] My influence lingers, which is disconcerting to Debbie who thinks I'm a ghost! In recent days I startled Debbie by appearing suddenly at her window. She could not understand the reason for my return until she realised that it was the first anniversary of her grandmother's death. She said to my owner 'Bosworth knows, he understands. He has come back as my comforter.'

The author, scholar and singer Peter Giles has many photographs from long ago of the great counter-tenor Alfred Deller, whom he saw in performance. For some years, Peter worked as a senior lay-clerk at Canterbury Cathedral where he told Maxine of having twice seen Deller's ghost: 'A seemingly supernatural presence.' He felt the power of the apparition standing behind him, and was impelled to turn towards this spirit. Peter said that he remembered Bernardo's words to Horatio on seeing the ghost of Hamlet's father: 'Is not this something more than fantasy?'

At the top of the stairs where I usually sleep, there is a large golden-framed portrait of the Galerie d'Apollon (a treasured memento of my scribe's winter birthday trip to Paris with her son Leon). When Henry James lay dying in his London rooms overlooking the Thames, his thoughts returned to his childhood visit to the Louvre's Napoleonic Galerie d'Apollon, where as a small boy he had experienced his dream/nightmare. Henry said that his 'real home was the Galerie d'Apollon'. In the first part of his autobiography he related this experience as 'the most appalling yet most admirable nightmare of my life'. During his last days, and in his final dictation, he entered an imaginative world connected to the beginning and end of his life as a writer. Mrs William James, his sister-in-law described the scene in her letters to her sons in America: 'He thinks he is voyaging and visiting foreign cities, and sometimes he asks for his glasses and paper and imagines that he writes. And sometimes his hand moves over the counterpane as if writing.'

James dictated a vision of himself as Napoleon and his own long-dead family members as the imperial Bonapartes. (I hope my impending senility doesn't take me to these psychopathic delusions.) Much as I admire Henry James *I* don't want any 'Napoleonic deathbed ramblings'. Viewing his body in the coffin at Carlyle Mansions, Miss Bosanquet wrote, 'Several people who have seen the dead face are struck with the likeness to Napoleon which is certainly great.' Henry James had a great sense of power and glory.

The grand images of terror and accomplishments that had stalked the long Galerie d'Apollon in his powerful 'dream-adventure' resonated with the Louvre as Napoleon's palace to which he had brought all the artistic treasures from his European conquests.

'Crossing the threshold of the Galerie d'Apollon, into the empire of his own creation, was for Henry James the crucial passage of his life and death,'[22] said the James scholar Leon Edel.

Another sublime space and threshold which 'embraces the highest poetical expression of Man and his Eternity' is Michelangelo's funeral chapel for the Medici family. It is dedicated to the Resurrection and depicts the transfiguration of death. It contains the tomb of the youthful, handsome Guilano, Duke of Nemours, and Lorenzo, Duke of Urbino.

The Chapel of the Medici

Below the sombre heroic statues of the two Medici are the disturbing beings of Night, Day, Dawn, and Dusk. *The Madonna with the Child* in the centre of the group is the spiritual focus of the elegiac Chapel, and the object of the gaze of the dead warrior dukes in antique armour, and the living priest saying the Mass for the repose of the souls of those buried there. The pensive Mary gently and lovingly holds the powerful body of the infant Jesus, which is spiralling upward away from her, into the light above. I admit that when I saw this image I was reminded of myself in youth, twisting and ascending in pursuit of a pigeon, performing a spectacular 'leap of death'. The words of the composer Geoffrey Burgon, on his own *Requiem* also came to mind: 'The image of an upward flight into nothingness.'

So much for human life and death, but what of cats and their Eternity?

'And when the body dissolves does anything at all remain of what we have called the soul? Or does nothing remain, and does our unquenchable desire for immortality spring, not from the fact that we are immortal, but from the fact that during the short span of our life we are in the service of something immortal?'

My scribe has just returned from a birthday trip to Rome with her daughter Tamsin. Like so many of their Victorian predecessors they used Nathaniel Hawthorne's evocative novel of murder and grace, *The Marble Faun,* as a tourist guidebook to Rome. They visited the Protestant Cemetery in Rome (known as the Cemetery of the Artists and Poets) where stray cats are exalted and lovingly cared for.

The marble faun of Praxiteles

The cats are regarded as the 'Guardians of the Departed' and appreciated for their 'silent presence'.

It is thought that their history is tightly entwined with that of the cemetery beneath the Aurelian wall, and that felines have occupied this 'walled-off, transported world at the bottom of the Aventine Hill', since the area was set aside as a non-Catholic burial ground in 1738, the date of the oldest tombstone. 'These feline guardians provide loyal companionship to the deceased, giving at the same time life and vitality to their resting-place,'[23] writes their modern benefactor, Matilde Talli.

As I grow older and anticipate my eighteenth birthday it seems that, like Henry James, I'm almost constantly in conversation or repose. He loved the Protestant Cemetery in Rome and spent many hours there quietly seated on a marble slab, walking with a companion, or talking to his deceased friends such as Constance Fenimore Woolson (1845-1894) buried in the oldest part by the 'time-silvered' Pyramid of Caius Cestius (first century BC), in the shadow of the dark cypresses and umbrella pines. Everyone's favourite sculpture seems to be William Wetmore Story's *The Angel of Grief*. Story was yet another American friend of Henry James. Inscriptions on antique Christian tombs sometimes represent conversations between the living and the dead.

> Faithful Gentianus in the peace of the Lord.
> He lived 21 years, 8 months and 16 days.
> In your prayers pray for us since we know that you are
> with Christ.
>
> Third Century Ad
> The Catacombs of Saint Callixtus

Apart from the atmosphere of antiquity in the beautiful little Cimitero Accatolico, he revered it as a place for expatriates. Henry

James was most touched by 'the appeal of the pious, English inscriptions among all these Roman memories'.

It pleases me that thanks to the efforts of Matilde Talli and her volunteers, the Cats of the Pyramid (how very Egyptian!) enjoy an elevated status each with his own 'green tangle of vegetation' and Roman sunlit turf 'overseen with pride'.

Her overwhelming financial burden in personally funding the feeding, neutering, and veterinary bills of all the Cats of the Pyramid, has recently been relieved by the Anglo-Italian Society for the Protection of Animals (AISPA). If you reader, would like to make a contribution to Matilde's work with the cemetery cats, it may be sent to:

AISPA
136 Baker Street
London W1U 6DU
(Attention: Cats of the
Protestant Cemetery, Rome)

The pyramid of Caius Cestius

And for further information, please contact Matilde Talli at
Tel: 06/5744136 or Cell 0339/2143222
http://www.igattidellapiramide.it
e-mail: info@igattidellapiramide.it

'Ye sleep in the Royal sepulchre of a bygone world, in the Pantheon of the human soul, the crumbling city walls of old Rome protect your shelter, and beyond, the Campagna spreads its vast silence around your dreams.'

(The words of Axel Munthe, writer and friend of Henry James. He is buried in the old part of the cemetery, known as the 'parte antica'.)

Tamsin visiting the cats of the pyramid

Things were not always this good for the non-Catholics and Cats of Rome. In the nineteenth century the moat which surrounded the *parte antica* was used for the deposition of dead cats and dogs. And until 1870 non-Catholics (let alone cats) were denied resurrection. All inscriptions indicating eternal bliss were strictly forbidden on non-Catholic tombstones, as the authorities believed that these might give the impression that there was a possibility for those outside the faith to gain eternal salvation.

The Orante, symbol of the soul in paradise

This denial of resurrection for non-Catholics has long since disappeared. Over the main entrance to the cemetery is a single word engraved in capital letters: 'RESURRECTURIS' (sanctified for those who shall rise again).

There is no evidence that Henry James petted the cats of the pyramid or that he believed in an afterlife for either humans or animals, but I think that his beautiful sentiments on this earthly paradise in Rome express my thoughts on the mystery of living and dying.

Bathed in the clear Roman light the place is heartbreaking for what it asks you – in such a world as this – to renounce. If it should 'make one in love with death, to be buried in so sweet a place' that's only if death should be conscious.[24]

When I heard on the news that the new leader of the Catholic Church loves felines, I decided to write to him and urge him to relieve the suffering of his fellow creatures on earth. Just as the non-Catholics in Rome had at last been accorded equal status in the hope of ascending to paradise, so the time had come for the Pope to intervene on behalf of the stray and feral Cats of Rome, not fortunate enough to be living either in the Protestant Cemetery, or Torre Argentina Cat Sanctuary near the Pantheon. Leon is thinking of working as a volunteer at this internationally renowned sanctuary. Animal welfare should be the responsibility of the State, and not rely solely on charities, excellent though they are. Also, the Vatican could direct some of its immense wealth towards homeless cats.

Cardinal Tarasio Bertone described Pope Benedict XVI as a man of science and of faith, and a cat lover: 'Every time he met a cat he would talk to it, sometimes for a long time…and the cat would follow him. Once about ten cats followed him into the Vatican and one of the Swiss Guards intervened, saying "Look, your eminence, the cats are invading the Holy See." '

There are estimated to be 150,000 stray cats in Rome. An army of cat ladies, called Gattari, leave them left-over pasta on street corners, but being a stray is still a hard life. Every year the cat sanctuary amidst the remains of four republic-era temples, hosts the Cat Pride parade. You can visit the cat sanctuary (close to the spot where Julius Caesar was slain) on a free guided tour organised by the volunteers each Sunday. You are welcome to contact the cat sanctuary at www.romancats.com, or telephone

06 687 21 33. Giuseppe Garibaldi (hero of our Conservative party leader David Cameron) founded the first animal protection society in Italy in 1871. Under the terms of the humane law of 1988 Roman cats are guaranteed the right to live where they are born.

Cardinal Roger Mahony, the Archbishop of Los Angeles has two silver tabbies, named Raphael and Gabriel. He believes that cats are perfect pets for clergymen 'because they are wonderful companions. There is almost a spirituality about them! Their presence is very soothing.'

Obviously, the present Pope agrees with the Cardinal, for he himself is the devoted owner of Chico, a black-and-white domestic shorthair (just like me!), who lives at the Pope's private residence in Bavaria. Agnes Heindl, housekeeper to the Pope's brother says, 'There's also a multi-coloured tabby cat that hangs around a lot of the time and keeps Chico company.'

Pets are not allowed in the Vatican, so he and Chico are separated for most of the time. As the Pope's 'love for cats is quite famous', and he must be heartbroken without his black and white feline companion, it seemed the perfect idea to amaze and delight him with my letter:

His Holiness Pope Benedict XVI
Vatican City
00817 Rome
Italy

June 4th 2006

Most Holy Father,

You are famous throughout the world as a *cat* person. I ask you to help relieve the plight of all the stray cats in Rome and throughout Italy, in every way you can. I've seen you on television on your balcony overlooking

St Peter's Square. We cats are also spiritual beings and prefer to be up high like the angels in Wim Wender's 'wings of desire', perched above bomb-ravaged Berlin. Have you seen this beautiful, melancholy film?

Firstly, it was an article on the internet 'The New Pope and the Pussycats' which emboldened me to address you, and secondly listening to a piece of music sung by the counter-tenor James Bowman and written by Alessandro Grandi in the 1620s in honour of your namesake St Benedict, 'O Beate Benedicte'.

O blessed Benedict,
blessed are those who gladly embrace your holy rule.
Blessed those who fly to your protection,
O blessed Benedict, intercede for us...

I understand that in Vatican City, described by some historians as 'the remains of the Roman Empire', you are thought of as a St Francis of Assisi or Dr Dolittle figure. I know that because of the absurd prohibition of cats in the Vatican you have had to leave your own dear Chico in Germany. You console yourself by feeding the strays in your beautiful private garden; you have been seen late at night. I think that you are the one to whom I can proclaim the miracle of my existence, the revelation that this letter is from a CAT – a black and white male just like your own dear one. I know that you believe in evolution and can be trusted to keep my 'literacy' a secret with the rigour of the confessional.

In conclusion I would like to be given a blessing and prayers for my improving health, and the alleviation of any symptoms of arthritis. I am currently working on my autobiography, and when it is published posthumously, a copy will be sent to you as a gift for your private library. I don't know the correct formula for saying goodbye to the Pope, so I'll end with a description of Henry James' feelings for his cousin Minny Temple, who died at the age of only twenty-four, before she could fulfil her dream of seeing England and Italy. 'A love as intense as "faith", passing through the senses into "mystery".'[25]

Bosworth of Little Leigh

Henry James loved his high-walled garden at Lamb House, especially an ancient mulberry tree which, to James' distress was felled by a sea-gale in January 1915. He wrote about the toppled tree in personal terms, '...once the fury of the tempest really descended he was bound to give way, because his poor old heart was dead, his immense old trunk was hollow.' Evergreen trees and shrubs in the garden of Lamb House lead to a small, secluded corner where you can find the graves of Henry James' dogs. He had a favourite dachshund, called Max, remembered with an elaborate tombstone.

The Vicar at Claybrooke Parva had a Pet Cemetery, but no such facility exists in this village. Little Leigh has had a succession of eccentric, sometimes dubious, or downright horrible Church of England vicars, who have certainly shown no concern for the burial of animals in consecrated ground.

The first in a catalogue of disastrous clergymen, 'an Oxford man' took 'early retirement' due to a breakdown, but in truth he was got rid of for 'bringing the Church of England into disrepute' and scrounging off the very parishioners he was supposed to serve. He clothed himself from the C of E jumble for charity and the 'dead box' at the local undertakers! There is a wonderful story told of how he complained of only *one* shoe having come from a corpse, only to be told that the deceased had had only one leg! He also wore ladies' lamé jumpers, and thumbed lifts to funerals! His true interest lay not in religion but in eating – so he was always especially enthusiastic about funerals – anticipating a big spread. His mission was not to comfort the bereaved, so much as downing the food of their relatives. This gluttony had reached a climax after the funeral of Brindie Granddad. The kindly driver of the hearse and the chief coffin-bearer linked arms with the vicar in order to bundle him in their car before he was able to pursue the mourners and their food. A scene from Francis Ford Coppola's *The Godfather* came to mind; appropriately it had been a favourite film of the deceased.

My scribe Maxine felt compassion for the 'foodie' vicar because he had been 'packed off' to a remote boarding school when only a small boy. He told us that it had been a terrible place where he had been bullied and abused and temporarily lost his belief in God. Another boy had been viciously bullied because he was Jewish; he had committed suicide by hanging himself from a school beam.

However, the vicar was a cat lover, having two of his own, named Magpie and Diogenes, and when he came to our house my female 'owner' always gave him a trayful of food, and afterwards I jumped onto his lap to be fussed. Sometimes he invited my family to go out for a meal saying 'this one's on me', but when it was time to pay he said that he had 'forgotten' his credit card.

A previous vicar was dismissed for stealing, and my friend (the ravenous one) was replaced by a dogmatic, conceited weirdo – a sort of Mr Collins figure from Jane Austen's *Pride and Prejudice*. At that time in my life I often strolled as far as the little village post office, almost opposite the farm where I was born. On one such occasion while sunning myself on a nearby area of grass, I overheard a conversation between Mrs D the evangelical Christian schoolmistress and an elderly parishioner. They were discussing the soon-to-be-installed, replacement vicar and speculating as to his suitability. When the elderly lady asked if (in contrast to his forbear) the new vicar was married, Mrs D said both defensively and approvingly, 'No, but he is a former member of the order of St John of the Cross,' as though those words alone must vanquish any doubts as to his appropriateness for Little Leigh. Of course, I took a different view and immediately suspected that he would be an authoritarian and discover a doctrine that condemned cats. Given that he originated from the strict organisation St John of the Cross, all I really know is that I wouldn't want to sit on his lap!

The Hindus say that with its last breath a spirit returns to the place it loves the best, there to remain for one day and night… . They apply this delightful belief to humans and animals. Let us hope that Henry James had his final twenty-four hours in the great gallery of Apollo before being reincarnated as a cat?!

The Greek immortals liked to look down from above. Mount Fengari (Mount Moon) is the highest mountain on the austere island of Samothrace, rising out of a landscape entirely of white marble. My scribe intends to visit it, taking with her Henry James' novel *The Wings of the Dove* which, like his memoir of her, immortalised the dead Minny Temple as 'the dove' Milly Theale, who would 'fly away and be at rest'. It was from the eminence of Mount Moon that Lord Poseidon sat to watch the progress of the Trojan War. Sitting there, after he had risen from the sea, he pitied the Greeks in their hour of defeat and was enraged with Zeus. So according to Homer's *Iliad*, Poseidon strode rapidly down the rocky slope as the hills and forests shook under the immortal feet of the descending god.

Winged Victory of Samothrace

It was in a rock niche nearby that the French discovered the famous *Winged Victory of Samothrace* and tore it from the grim sanctuary of the great (Cabeiric gods). They stole this pagan angel and placed it in the Louvre. The Greek Nikes were the forerunners of Christian angels.

I've just learned (and it's a chilling recollection) that in their shrines to fertility, immortality and eternal youth, pale-coloured animals were offered to the heavens, but black animals were sacrificed to the gods of the Underworld. How would I have been classified by these ancient Greeks?

Is there anything more beautiful than white marble in moonlight? I've seen just such a photograph of the Taj Mahal, an elegy in marble to love eternal and Mumtaz Mahal (the choice of the realm), or some say an expression of a 'dream'. According to Dan Cruickshank in his book *Around the World in 80 Treasures*, the sounds inside the Taj Mahal 'the sobbing and sighing of the stones' are like an eternal lament. 'The Taj Mahal carries in its geometry a powerful message about life, death and rebirth… . It makes death tangible and the grief of Shah Jahan eternal…death dwells in a carapace of serene geometric beauty.'[26]

According to Lawrence Durrell, the Greeks adopted the Cypress tree 'as a symbol of the immortal soul and equally of eternal death…'. They also used it as coffin-wood for Greek heroes and for the masts of their war ships. 'It is curious that something which, to the peoples of the east expressed only joy and beauty should, in coming west, become associated with death and the afterlife.'[5]

On Peckham Rye, as a child of eight or ten perhaps, William Blake had his 'first vision'. Sauntering along, he looked up and saw an angel in a tree, what Peter Ackroyd describes as 'the English penchant for the dream and the vision'. I find this combination of tree and serene messenger particularly appealing.

In life, cats love to be seated on high, surveying their kingdom. I know that the time will come when, like the cat Hendrix, dedicatee of this book, I'll be buried underneath a favourite tree,

The Taj Mahal

in the simplicity of my own back garden. But I also know that ancestral voices will call to me as they did to my predecessor Tom, and I'll become what the Greeks termed the Katascopos (the one who saw from above). In suspended ecstasy I'll look down on the beautiful earth below – still full of happiness.

When my body dies,
Let my soul be given
The glory of Paradise

Angel in a tree

Postscript

On Sunday the 20th August 2006 as evening rain began to fall, Bosworth refused to enter the house for his usual mealtime. He looked very frail and unwell; I noticed yet more bloodspots in his golden hyper-expressive eyes. Stubbornly remaining outside in the porch, and having heard me again approach to open the front door and call him in, he decided to run off unseen to one of those secret places of the earth.

The Friday afternoon prior to his vanishing and Tamsin's departure for a weekend in Lincolnshire, Bosworth sat on the keyboard in Leon's computer room, manically kneading, miaowing, and purring. Having rolled upside down for over an hour, he again began to kneed the keyboard incoherently, whilst Tamsin stroked him and tried to continue typing. When she returned from Lincoln on Monday to discover Bosworth gone, it seemed to her that during that last contented Friday afternoon, he had perhaps been saying goodbye.

It was the belief of the ancient Greeks that the newly dead visit their loved ones in dreams. The shade of Patroclus appears to the exhausted Achilles, as he lies asleep on the shore.

Almost a week after his disappearance I'm waiting for Bosworth to come to me in my sleep. He'll tell me what happened before 'he passed the Gates of the Sun and the regions of dreams', and where to find him.

A CKNOWLEDGEMENTS

Grateful acknowledgement to Leon Handy for preliminary typesetting and design.

My thanks to the following publishers, authors and organisations for allowing me to use quotes from their books and resources.

1   At the Grave of Henry James, from *Collected Poems* by W H Auden. Reproduced with permission of the publishers Faber and Faber Ltd.

2   Beryl Bainbridge – from an article in *The Times* (2004).

3   The Notebooks of Leonardo da Vinci.

4   From *The Portable Nietzsche* by Friedrich Nietzsche, edited by Walter Kaufmann, translated by Walter Kaufmann, copyright 1954 by the Viking Press, renewed ©1982 by Viking Penguin Inc. Used by permission of Viking Penguin, a division of Penguin Group (USA) Inc.

5   *The Greek Islands*, by Lawrence Durrell (1978). Reproduced with permission of the publishers Faber and Faber Ltd.

6   *The Odyssey* by Homer (p145) translated by E V Rieu and D C H Rieu (Penguin Classics 1946, Revised edition 1991). Copyright 1946 by E V Rieu. This revised translation copyright ©the Estate of the late E V Rieu, and D C H Rieu, 1991. Introduction and Index and Glossary copyright ©Peter V Jones, 1991. Reproduced by permission of Penguin Books Ltd

7   Ella Hepworth Dixon on Henry James.

8   F M Hueffer on Henry James.

9   Violet Hunt, Henry James and the Cat on his lap anecdote.

10 Thomas Hobbes, *The Leviathan* (1651), published in Pelican Books 1968, reprinted 1971.

11 Carlo Gesualdo da Venosa (1560-1613).

12 An excerpt from a madrigal by Carlo Gesualdo, performed by counter-tenor Alfred Deller in 1959. Reissued on Vanguard Classics, 1994.

13 Nikos Kazantzakis.

14 Charlotte Brontë.

15 The Notebooks of Leonardo da Vinci.

16   Nikos Kazantzakis.

17   E Schrödinger, *What is Life? Mind and Matter* (1967). Reproduced by kind permission of Cambridge University Press.

18   Jellicle Cats, from *Old Possum's Book of Practical Cats*, by T S Eliot. Reproduced with permission of the publishers Faber and Faber Ltd.

19   Dr Annemarie Schimmel's introduction to Lorraine Chittock's book *Cairo Cats – Egypt's Enduring Legacy*. Reproduced with the kind permission of Dr Annemarie Schimmel and Lorraine Chittock.

20   *Journey out of Essex*, John Clare (1841) from *John Clare By Himself*, edited by Eric Robinson and David Powell. Published by Routledge in 2002.

21   Lewis Carroll, *Alice's Adventures in Wonderland*, Penguin Popular Classics, 1994.

22   Henry James: *A Life* Reprinted by permission of HarperCollins Publishers Ltd. ©Leon Edel (1985).

23   Matilde Talli's booklet on the Cats of the Protestant Cemetery in Rome. By kind permission of Matilde Talli and AISPA (The Anglo-Italian Society for the Protection of Animals).

24   *The Selected Letters of Henry James*, ed Leon Edel. The Belknap Press of Harvard University Press, Cambridge, Massachusetts.

25 *The Autobiography of Henry James*, ed F W Dupree. W H Allen, London, 1956.

26 *Around The World in 80 Treasures*, by Dan Cruickshank (2005). Reproduced by Permission of Weidenfeld and Nicholson, a division of The Orion Publishing Group.

PICTURE CREDITS

1 NATIONAL PICTURES. The large sculpture, *The Writer*, by Italian artist Giancarlo Neri on Hampstead Heath in north London. © TopFoto/National News.

2 *Page of Cats* (1513-16), Leonardo da Vinci. Pen and ink and wash, Windsor Castle Royal Library. © Her Majesty Queen Elizabeth II.

3 Detail of Chapel of St Hubert doorway, Amboise. © 2004 TopFoto.

4 How to talk to your cat – advertisement in *The Independent* newspaper.

5 *Portrait of Henry James* by John Singer Sargent, National Portrait Gallery, London

6 Caduceus: a Doctor's sign, Wellcome Library, London.

7   *Portrait of Benjamin Britten* (photo), Haags
    Gemeentemuseum, The Hague, Netherlands. Bridgeman
    Art Library.

8   *Henry Wriothesley, 3rd Earl of Southampton* (1573-1624), 1603
    (oil on canvas) by John de Critz, the Elder (c.1552-1642)
    (attr. to), Boughton House, Northamptonshire, UK.
    Bridgeman Art Library.

9   Tamsin and Leon at school. Reproduced with the kind
    permission of Tempest Photography, St Ives, Cornwall.

10 Schrödinger's cat experiment: *Schrödinger's Cat*. Computer
    graphic depicting the famous 'Schrödinger's Cat' thought
    experiment, showing a cat (both dead and alive) inside a
    box with a vial of poison and a radioactive trigger. In this
    hypothetical situation, the cat is thought to be both alive
    and dead until observed. This is because a quantum event
    (the decay of a radioactive particle) is set up to trigger the
    release of a lethal poison that kills the cat. According to
    quantum physics, the unstable particle exists in an
    intermediate 'probabilistic' state until it is observed. The
    Austrian physicist Erwin Schrödinger devised this
    experiment to demonstrate the bizarre philosophical
    implications of quantum theory.
    MEHAU KULYK/SCIENCE PHOTO LIBRARY

11 Interior view of the Galerie d'Apollon (photo) by French
    School (seventeenth century) Louvre, Paris, France. Lauros/
    Giraudon. Bridgeman Art Library.

12 *Dusk and Dawn* from the Tomb of Lorenzo de Medici,
    designed 1521, carved 1524-34 (marble) by Michelangelo

Buonarroti (1475-1564), New Sacristy, San Lorenzo, Florence, Italy. Bridgeman Art Library.

13   *Statue of the Faun*, copied from Praxitiles, in the Vatican Museums, Vatican City. © Alinari Archives – Anderson Archives, Florence. TopFoto.

14   *Female Orant between two shepherds*, late third century (fresco) by Paleo-Christian (third century) Cimitero Maggiore, Rome, Italy, ©Held Collection, Bridgeman Art Library.

15   *The Winged Victory of Samothrace* (Parian marble), Greek, (second century BC), Louvre, Paris, France. Bridgeman Art Library.

16   *View of the Taj Mahal*, built by Emperor Shah Jahan (1592-1666), completed in 1643, photo by Ustad Ahmad Lahori Agra, India. Bridgeman Art Library.

17   Angel in a tree.

All other photographs were taken by the family and friends of Bosworth and are reproduced with their kind permission. A special thank you to John Chilton of Canada for the photographs taken at Lamb House in summer 2006.

Every reasonable effort has been made to trace and acknowledge the ownership of the copyrighted material in this book. Any errors or omissions that may have occurred are inadvertent, and will be corrected in subsequent editions provided notification is sent to the publisher.